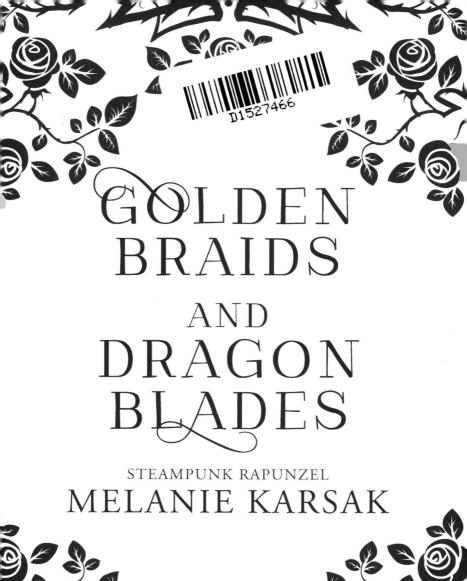

GOLDEN BRAIDS
AND
DRAGON BLADES

STEAMPUNK RAPUNZEL

MELANIE KARSAK

Golden Braids and Dragon Blades: Steampunk Rapunzel

Steampunk Fairy Tales
Clockpunk Press, 2018

Published by Clockpunk Press
Editing by Becky Stephens Editing
Proofreading by Rare Bird Editing
Proofreading by Siren Editing
Cover art by Art by Karri

for Esra and Evren

THIS BOOK BELONGS TO:

_____

GOLDEN BRAIDS

AND
DRAGON BLADES

PROLOGUE
GOTHEL

I stood in the dark under the shadow of the hazel tree. Through the window of their second-floor apartment situated above the fishmonger's shop, I saw her pace the small flat. She wouldn't be able to see me, just like he—the *father*, if you could call him that—had not when he'd come to steal from my garden. I shook my head. Such low people. I fingered the amulet hanging from my neck, a slim metal shard dangling from a braid of silver hair.

I watched her as I had done these nine long months. She was tall and lanky, her brown curls stuffed up under a scarf. She wore an apron over a drab brown dress. Only her massive stomach, protruding like an infection, gave her body any shape. She walked back and forth across the small space, cursing like a sailor, then put one finger to one nostril and blew her nose onto the floor.

I squeezed the amulet in my hand, feeling the metal dig into my palm.

Are you sure? Are you sure this—this—*is sacred blood?*

The metal grew hot in my hand.

I sighed.

The door slapped open.

"Oi, Deloris. You here, dove?" Craig—the *father*—called when he entered their one-room flat.

Dove? I rolled my eyes.

"Where have you been?" she asked, slapping him on the head. "I'm worn through. I'm about to take a knife and cut this lump outta me. You get it?"

He lifted a cloth bag, opening it to reveal the bundle of rapunzel he'd filched from my garden. Deloris grabbed the bag from his hand and began eating it at once.

"You see 'er?"

Craig shook his head. "No. Crotchety old witch, probably asleep. I snuck there and back no problem."

"Go again tomorrah. Understand? God, I hope this thing gets out of me soon," she said, swatting her swollen stomach.

I clenched my jaw at the sight, reminding myself not to do something rash—at least not until the child was born. I squeezed the amulet once more.

"Any luck with his lordship?" she asked, her mouth full of my greens.

Craig rubbed his hands together. "He said that if it's got a cock and balls, he'll take it. You hear that?" Craig said, shouting at his wife's protruding belly. "You better be growing the right equipment, or we're just going to let the Thames have you."

"Could sell it to a brothel if it's a girl."

"Enough bastards at a brothel. Might as well just leave it in the woods."

"Lord, I'm so hungry!" Deloris said, shoving handfuls of the rapunzel into her mouth. "Make sure you go back tomorrah."

"You already said that. Might not be any more growing by then."

"Witch's garden always has a fresh batch by mornin'."

"Witch," Craig said with a laugh. "Half-deaf old hag. A steamcar could roll through her backyard, and she'd never hear."

They both laughed.

I turned and looked at my garden. Craig had trampled my basil in his not-so-subtle attempt at thievery. I frowned then waved my hand over the plants, a shimmer of silver gliding from my fingers. The basil righted once more, springing back to its upright position. As the glimmer of magic cascaded to the soil, a new row of rapunzel sprouted to life. The large, leafy greens would be ready by morning.

I rolled the amulet around my fingers then gazed back up at the window. Deloris and Craig were now bickering. I eyed the woman's belly.

The ninth generation. That's what Merlin had promised so long ago. I hoped he was right, because I was tired and done with this world. I looked overhead as an airship floated past. An airship. I shook my head. I was most definitely done with this world. Sighing, I turned and headed back inside.

It was the scream in the middle of the night two days later that woke me. I'd fallen asleep in the chair that looked out at their apartment. I rose, leaning against my staff, and went to the window. There was a flurry of activity inside.

Deloris was cursing.

Craig flung himself to and fro in an annoyed huff then rushed out the flat door.

I closed my eyes and twisted my hands. Magic rolled from my fingertips. A glimmer of pink light moved from my fingers and across the garden between my cottage to their tiny apartment. It slipped in through the window unseen. It seemed like forever until her screaming abated. It would go more comfortably for her now.

Closing my eyes, I waited and listened. It seemed like time had stopped. Finally, I heard it. A single shrill cry rang through the night.

My teacup sitting in its saucer clattered as it shifted across the table. The windowpanes rattled.

I opened my eyes and stared through the window.

A few moments later, Craig flung open the door, and he and the surgeon appeared.

"By Christ, Deloris. If you were just going to birth the thing yourself, I wouldn't have fetched the surgeon. Now I have to pay him. Boy or girl?"

I listened hard but couldn't hear her answer.

"Dammit!" Craig exclaimed, running his fingers through his hair.

Girl.

The surgeon bent, disappearing out of sight. A few moments later, he rose holding a squalling bundle. The tiny screams had attracted an owl who alighted in my hazel tree. And then another and another. I watched as they all gathered. The bats, the raccoons, the creatures of the night. All were drawn by the baby's cries.

I would need to get her away from here. Away from everyone. Anyone who saw her—even people as rude as Deloris and Craig—would eventually notice the child was special. If they didn't drown her first.

Craig handed the surgeon some coin, and the man departed.

I turned and looked around the room. The key to my small cottage lay on the table nearby. A glint of moonlight shimmered on it.

I nodded. "Very well."

Opening my bag, I waved my hand at my few precious belongings, lifting them with magic, directing them to my bag. I grabbed my key and turned and headed outside.

I ambled around the block toward the fishmonger's shop. As I neared the gaslamps, the flames whispered to me, telling me what must be done.

Merlin was right after all. We just needed to wait and watch. Now, she had come.

The surgeon, carrying his medical bag, walked through the foggy air down the cobblestone away from the building, muttering under his breath.

I cast a glance up at the owls perched on the rooftop of the building.

"Get hence," I whispered, waving a hand at them. "Before someone notices you."

They hooted loudly and flew off. But they didn't go far. Large yellow eyes watched from the shadows of the trees nearby.

As I rounded the building, the stink of fish assailed my nostrils.

I went to the door leading to the flat upstairs and slowly climbed the steps. I could hear the baby crying and Craig cursing.

"And just what are we going to do now?" Craig demanded.

"I'm tired. Shut it," Deloris snapped.

I knocked on the door.

"What was that?" Deloris asked.

"Probably someone to come complain about all the noise," Craig replied then opened the door. "Look—" he began but stopped when he saw me.

"Well, what is it?" Deloris asked. "Oh, you, quiet down, girl," she added, scolding the newborn baby.

Craig stepped back, and I entered the room slowly. I eyed

Craig. He was a drunk and thief, nothing more. I turned to Deloris. Just under her skin, I saw the shimmer of something that lay dormant in her blood. She merely carried the seed; she was nothing. When my eyes went to the child, however, I saw the rosy pink glow all around her. Fools, couldn't they see it too?

Deloris rocked the child far too roughly as she glared at me. "Well, what do you want?" she finally asked.

"The child," I answered simply.

"The child?" Craig asked with a laugh. "Get out of here before I beat you."

"You grew that child with my rapunzel. Shall I tell the constables how you stole from my garden?"

Craig sneered. "Another word out of you, witch, and I'll bury you in that garden."

I smirked then twisted my fingers, calling forth a sparkle around my fingertips. "I would like to see you try."

"Craig," Deloris whispered. Wide-eyed, she looked from Craig to me.

"What about a trade?" I asked.

"Trade? Trade what?" Craig asked.

I opened my palm, showing them the key lying therein. "My house for your child."

The two exchanged a glance then Craig quickly crossed the room and grabbed the bundle from his wife, who shoved it in his direction.

"No tricks," he said, eyeing me warily.

"No tricks. It is a pact. The child for the house. A binding agreement," I replied.

He met my eye. "A binding agreement?"

"You understand me." From the expression on his face, he did. Breaking a deal with a witch—or so they thought me—would result in death.

"I agree," he said then handed the child to me, snatching the key from my hand. Smiling from ear to ear, he raced back to his wife and began helping her from the bed.

The tiny bundle in my arms wriggled and cried.

"Sleep, little one," I said, soothing her. The little baby opened her eyes and squinted at me. Even then I could see her eyes were a kaleidoscope of shifting colors. I gently set my hand on her brow, setting a sweet charm of sleep on her.

The baby sighed contentedly then dozed off.

I turned and headed back outside. Rushing down the cobblestone, I made my way to the airship towers. As I did so, I shed the rumpled cloak I wore. Tossing my walking stick into a garden—it quickly morphed back into the form of a hazel tree —I shifted my shape. My features firmed, the lines on my face disappearing as I transformed into a woman in her twenties with dark hair wearing an elegant blue gown and fashionable mini top hat. Even as I walked, I felt my breasts fill with milk. I touched the rags covering the baby. They shifted to a delicate gown, bonnet, and blanket.

I went to the pilot's station. One sleepy guard and one sleeping airship captain waited.

I cleared my throat politely.

"Oh, pardon, madame. We weren't expecting anyone at this hour," the guard said as he wiped tears of fatigue from his cheeks.

"I need a transport."

"Liam, get up," the guard said, kicking the cot on which the captain slept. "Where to, madame?"

"Cornwall."

"Got silver?"

I shook my bag, the coins inside jangling.

The pilot rose, adjusted his shirt. "All right, lady. Let's go. My God, what a little one you have there. Boy or girl?"

"Girl."

"She got a name?"

I smiled down at the bundle sleeping soundly in my arms. "Rapunzel."

1
ZOETROPE

"Rapunzel, let down your hair," Mother called in singsong from below. I went to the entrance of the cave, which was situated high on the cliff side, and set my eye on the telescope. The end of the telescope poked just outside a waterfall of vines and roots that covered the entrance to my home in the seawall.

Which I never left.

Ever.

Mother stood on the sandy beach below.

Grabbing my strawberry blond locks, I shoved aside the curtain of ivy and roots and looped my braided tresses around a hook on the cave wall. I waved to Mother then dropped my hair. My long locks tumbled to the beach below.

Mother smiled. In a glimmer of sparkling light, she shifted form to that of a child. Spider-like, she crawled up my braid like it was a ladder.

As I stood waiting, I gazed out at the waters of the English Channel. The dark blue waters pitched and rolled. Light scattered on the water's surface making it shine. The foamy white caps broke against the beach. It was low tide. When the tide rolled in, there wouldn't even be any beach there. No one would ever suspect that someone lived in a cave nearby.

I closed my eyes and felt the wind on my face. I imagined, not for the first time, what it would be like to ride in one of the airships that flew overhead. I imagined how thrilling it would be to race through the clouds. I also imagined what it would be like to ride a horse, galloping across a field full of wildflowers. Like the knights in all the old Arthurian tales, I imagined chasing down some dangerous criminal on my fleet-footed charger. The wind caressing my cheek, I imagined racing down the streets of London in a steam-powered auto, my hands gripping the wheel as I took the turns at high speeds. I imagined everything. Because what else could I do but imagine?

I sighed.

The wind chimes made of shells and silver bells just inside my cave tinkled in the sea breeze.

Imagining was all I would ever do. There was no life for me outside this cave.

I felt the tension on my hair ease as Mother reached the cave.

"Good morning," she called merrily. "And what are you dreaming about, love?" she asked.

I opened my eyes in time to see her shift back into the woman I knew: a tall, dark-haired, regal beauty. Sheltered as I was, I still knew she was striking. Unlike me. I was a lump of unmolded clay covered in hair that never seemed to stop growing. I cast a glance down at my clothes. Dressed in a worn petticoat embroidered on the hem, but still two sizes too short, and an old but comfortable corset, I was anything but regal. Not that it mattered. No one ever saw me anyway. I was entirely frumpy. Well, except for my eyes. Mother always told me my eyes were special. Kaleidoscope eyes. That's what she called them, the colors in my eyes turning and shifting with my emotions. Mother said that my eyes were so unique that if the wrong person saw me, they might want to harm me. So I stayed in my cave whether I wanted to or not. I stayed in my cave, so my eyes wouldn't get me killed.

"Nothing," I answered with a sigh. I cast a glance back at the periwinkle blue sky. One day, maybe, kaleidoscope eyes or no, I would ride an airship. One day, I would find a way.

I unhooked my hair and pulled it back inside. Coiling it into a massive heap at my nape, I removed the hairpins I'd stuck into the top of my bodice and wove them back into my strawberry blonde locks. My hair shimmered almost copper-colored in the sunshine.

"I come bearing gifts," Mother said as she started unpacking the satchel she wore. "Thought they might cheer you."

"Thank you," I said, turning reluctantly away from the view. My mind clung to my imaginary adventures, unwilling to let them go. "But you know what would cheer me most?" For once, I hoped she would say yes. To anything, any adventure *outside* the cave. But I knew even before the words left my lips that there was no hope.

"I do indeed, but it cannot be helped. You know that, my dear," Mother said as she set parcels on the table.

"I know, but maybe…maybe I could just go swimming. You know, not far, just at the base of the sea wall. I could use a rope ladder to get up and down. I'd only go at low tide, so it would be safe."

"But you have a pool of water in the lower portion of the cave."

"Yes, but it's not big enough for swimming. And you can't see the sky there."

Mother turned and set her hand on my cheek. "Rapunzel," she said lovingly. "Come see what I brought you." Taking me by the hand, she led me to a table. I bit my tongue, well aware she was attempting to turn the conversation. It was no use. No matter what I said, the answer was always no. Instead, I turned my attention to Mother's gifts. On the table, I found three books and a box. A sweet-smelling parcel was sitting on my makeshift kitchen counter.

"What's this?" I asked, lifting the box.

"Open it," she said with a smile.

I lifted the lid on the box and from within, pulled out a device that looked a bit like a lantern. The machine was made of paper. Small slits were cut into the sides. On the inside, around the entire circumference, was a row of dragon silhouettes. At the center, there was an unlit candle. "What is it?"

"They call it a zoetrope," she said. "Watch." She gave the device a spin.

As the paper spun, it created an illusion. The dragons took flight and began breathing fire. I clasped my hands together and lifted them to my lips. Slowly, the zoetrope stopped spinning, and the dragons rested once more.

"Delightful!"

Mother grinned. "At night, when it's dark, take it to the back and light the candle at the center. Then give it a spin. Through these slats, the dragons will be reflected on the walls."

"I love it," I said, wrapping my arms around Mother's waist.

"I thought you would," she said then kissed me on the head. She sighed heavily then hugged me close. When she did so, I felt the tension in her body. Though she'd been all mirth and smiles, something had her on edge. She kissed me on the head once more, then went back to the cave entrance and looked into the telescope. She scanned up and down the beach.

"Mother, what is it?"

"Nothing, dear," she said. "Where are they?"

I pointed toward the back of the cave. "Sleeping."

"Have they been out?"

"Not since last night. Mother? Is anything the matter?"

She stepped away from the telescope. "Of course not," she said with a smile, but I saw the twitch at the corner of her mouth that told me she wasn't telling the complete truth. "Shall we have a treat? I brought cherry tarts from the baker." She pointed to a bakery box on the counter.

I eyed her carefully. "All right." I moved the zoetrope aside to make a space for us to eat then went to the cupboard from which I pulled out two pretty plates, one with pink roses and the other in blue and white with a picture of lovers sitting in a garden. I stroked my finger across the image of the boy and held in the sigh that wanted to escape my lips. Setting the table, I placed the plates, cloth napkins, and a fork and knife out for us.

Mother leaned against the side of the cave entrance. Staring out through the vines, she played with the little metal charm she always wore.

"Tea?" I asked.

"Yes, please," she said absently.

I set out two cups and saucers then went to the small stove, more a hole in the cave wall than an oven, and grabbed the teapot that had been hanging over the embers.

Eyeing Mother closely, I poured the tea, set the pot aside, then opened the bakery box. I breathed in the rich smells of sugar, butter, dough, and cherries. Gingerly, I set the tarts on the plates.

"Ready," I called.

Still lost in her thoughts, Mother delayed a moment then turned and came to the table.

"*Bon appétit*," she said.

"*Merci beaucoup*," I replied.

"*Tres bien*," she said with a smile.

"I've been studying."

Mother smiled lightly then spooned sugar—five teaspoons —into her cup. I settled for a single dollop of honey.

We ate in silence. The chime hanging just inside the cave jangled in the soft sea breeze.

From the back, we heard a soft sneeze.

Both Mother and I turned and looked, but they weren't awake yet. Slugabeds.

"I want you to keep them in for the next few days," Mother said lightly as if the request was nothing to be alarmed about.

Staring at her, I set down my fork. "Why?"

"Just a precaution."

I swallowed hard. "Is something wrong?"

Mother sat back in her chair. "No. There are just rumors, that's all. Probably nothing. We just want to make sure you're safe. I need to leave again this afternoon. I might not be back for a few days. Just keep them in until I return."

I stared at her. "All right. What kind of rumors?"

Mother reached across the table and squeezed my hand. "Nothing to worry about. I just need to make sure all is well and that rumors are just that. Now, did you see what books I brought you?"

I frowned, knowing full well Mother wasn't being honest with me.

Smiling at me over her teacup, she motioned to the books.

Tipping my head, I looked at the spines. "*The Tale of Culhwch and Olwen*. I don't have that one." I picked up the book. Another Arthurian tale. Always Arthurian tales. At this point, I had all of them practically memorized.

"That is a very old one. It's about a knight named Culhwch who wants to win the love of Olwen, whose father was a giant."

"That must not have gone easily."

Mother laughed. "Most definitely not."

"Does he succeed?"

"Read and find out."

I ran my hand across its bright red leather binding. The

title had been embossed with golden letters, around which were roses and vines. I was surprised there was still an Arthurian tale I hadn't read. Every knight, every lady seemed like old friends.

I studied the other books. "*Pride and Prejudice* by Jane Austen. Oh! Is this a romance?" I cracked open the book at once. While Mother insisted I read every old legend ever written, what I most craved were modern romances.

Mother nodded. "The bookseller said lovely things about that one. Very popular. I'm told all the young ladies read Miss Austen's works."

I nodded, thinking about *all the young ladies*. I had seen engravings of those young ladies in the newspapers Mother sometimes brought. The images of those beautiful ladies in fine dresses and carrying parasols gave me a glimpse of a life I'd never have. I'd never go to a ball. Or walk around the gardens on some fine estate. Or go on a picnic. Or have a proper high tea. Or meet some fine man's mother and sister. I'd never take a trip to Bath or see an opera. I'd never do anything *all the young ladies* do. Nor would I be like the lady airship captains in their trousers and goggles. Their lives seemed far more adventurous than those of *all the young ladies* and very exciting. But I'd never be like them either, hanging on to ropes and barking orders to my crew. No. I was destined to live and die in a cave like some hobgoblin.

Mother picked up the last tome. Grinning, she handed it to me. "And *Don Juan* by Lord Byron," she said.

"Lord Byron? Wasn't he that scandalous poet who was the lover of Lily Stargazer, the famous airship racer?"

"Yes, he was. I thought his work might stir your…imagination," she said with a playful smirk.

I raised my eyebrows and opened the book. Inside was a painting of the poet with his curly dark hair, pouty lips, and pale blue eyes. "Well, Lord Byron, we'll have to see what you're on about," I said, eyeing the poet. He really had been very handsome.

Mother chuckled.

We ate quietly. When we were done, I rose to clear the dishes, but Mother motioned for me to sit.

"Have another tea," she said, kissing me on the head once more.

She took all the plates and set them in the wash bin. Working quickly, she washed them up and set them aside to dry. She dried off her hands then went to the opening of the cave once more. She looked out through the vines then sighed.

"I need to go," she said. Turning back to me, she smiled, but I saw that odd little tremor at the corner of her mouth again. And she was fingering her amulet in earnest once more. "Everyone stays until I say, all right?"

"They won't like it."

She nodded. "I know, and I'm sorry for it. I'll make it up to them."

"Might be hard to convince Wink."

"Talk to her. She'll listen to you."

I chuckled then rolled my eyes at the impossibility of the task.

"Well, try, at least," Mother said with an understanding grin.

I joined her at the cave entrance. Pulling out the pins that held my hair, I stuffed them into the ripped seam at the top of my corset. I lifted my long braid, getting ready to hook it, but Mother motioned for me to wait. Putting her eye to the telescope, she scanned the beach again.

A sick feeling rocked my stomach. Something wasn't right. Mother wasn't saying what, but clearly more than rumors were afoot.

"Mother?" I whispered.

She leaned back and nodded to me. "All clear. Go ahead, if you please," she said, motioning to my braid.

I wound my hair around the hook, letting the long braid fall to the sandy beach below.

Mother hugged me once more. As she held me, she whispered, "Just stay inside Merlin's cave, my love. You're safe here. Everyone stays inside, all right?"

"Yes."

"Promise?"

"I promise."

"Very good. I'll be back soon," she said then stepped back. Working her fingers, a sparkle of magic glimmered on her fingertips. She shifted into a child once more. "I love you," she said, her voice high and sweet.

I giggled. "I love you too."

She winked at me then swiftly climbed back down my hair. When she reached the bottom, I felt a light tug.

Unhooking my hair, I pulled my braid back inside. The end was wet and covered in sand. I lifted the hair to my nose and inhaled deeply, smelling the salty sea spray and sandy beach, then I turned and headed back into my cave.

2
THE THREE SISTERS

I LAY ON MY COT LISTENING TO WATER DRIP FROM THE ROCKS somewhere in the back of the cave. A storm had blown in that afternoon, and it had been raining in earnest all day and night since Mother had left. Wherever she was, I hoped Mother was warm and dry. And safe.

I tapped my finger on the book lying on my chest in time to the dripping water. My mind swirled around thoughts of Jane Austen's Mister Darcy. What a brooding, insufferable, and wholly enticing creature. No wonder *all the young ladies* liked Miss Austen's book. It was enchanting, as was Mister Darcy. I set my finger on my lips, stroking them gently.

I would never leave this cave.

I would never meet a man.

I would never be kissed.

I would live and die here.

Alone.

I heard a soft chirp then a little head nuzzled under my chin, wiggling into the warm spot between my chin and chest.

Well, not entirely alone.

I opened my eyes to find a golden tail sticking out from

under one side of my chin, a tiny snout sticking out of the other, legs and feet on my chest.

I slid my fingers to her belly and tickled her tummy, eliciting a puff of smoke. She chirped happily, which got the attention of her sisters. Soon, two more little bodies crawled over me looking for warm spots to lie in.

I sat up, removing Estrid from my neck and setting her on my lap. I gazed down at the three little creatures staring expectantly at me. Estrid, realizing she had lost her comfy spot, huffed in annoyance and flew off. After one turn around the room, she landed on the nearby ledge and sneezed, blasting off a tiny puff of fire, which briefly illuminated the room with bright orange light and made her golden scales shimmer.

"Don't get huffy," I told her with a grin. "I needed to sit up, and dragons don't make good scarves."

Estrid snorted at me.

I gazed down at Luna. In the dim candlelight, her opalescent, pale blue and silver scales shimmered softly. She gazed at me with her beady dark eyes. I rubbed her under her chin.

"What is it, Luna?"

She rubbed her head into the palm of my hand.

"Pet me, pet me, pet me, eh? Luna-lay, Lula-lu, Luna-li," I sang as I stroked her head, which elicited happy chirps from the kitten-sized dragon.

Jealous of the attention her sisters were getting, Wink batted her colorful wings. The rainbow of colors thereon, more reminiscent of a butterfly than any dragon I'd ever read about, fluttered gracefully.

"Oh, jealous girl," I said, giving Wink a pat. "I see you. Well, everyone ready?" I asked. Setting Miss Austen's book aside, I slipped off the bed. The dragons lifted up on their tiny wings, excited to see what adventure I had in store for them tonight.

I grinned at them. "You *sure* you're ready?"

Estrid eyed me carefully, watching each little twitch of my muscles. When I flicked my eyes to the left, she looked left. When I flicked my eyes right, she looked right. I lifted a finger on my left hand; her muscles tensed left. Grabbing a small pillow, I tossed it at the willful little dragon to distract her then took off, running as fast as I could run toward the labyrinth of tunnels in the back of the cave.

And we were off.

Moving quickly in my bare feet, I slipped through the narrow gap in the rocks in my so-called library and into the elaborate cave network. The cave, lit only by an occasional lantern refracted with mirrors throughout the tunnels—a pretty clever invention of my own design—was an intricate network of tunnels and chambers, and it was our favorite place to play. Of course, the play was more for them than me. Each sister was no bigger than a cat, with Luna, the youngest, no bigger than a kitten. Given they didn't go out except at night, their wings needed exercise. As it was, I wanted to distract them from the fact that they wouldn't be going outside tonight.

I rushed over the boulder where the tunnel split, then wound down toward the chamber at the bottom of the cave network. A blast of orange light behind me told me Estrid was close.

But then I felt a hum in the air and a moment later, Wink appeared before me.

I laughed. "Show off."

I felt the hum of magic once more and true to her name, the dragon winked then disappeared. A moment later, she called tauntingly from the chamber below. Luna and Estrid darted past me as they too headed to the sea chamber.

I reached the chamber a few moments behind them. Below, the pool of water swirled. The sea organisms living below the waves made the water come alive with blue light. I sat down on the ledge and watched the dragons. Estrid and Luna were perched on the stalactites hanging from the cave ceiling. Wink was on the single stalagmite at the center of the pool, the unicorn horn, or so I'd named it. Keeping quiet, I watched as the three dragons scanned the water, their eyes on the fish therein. They called to one another, a series of click and chirps, and then they worked.

Wink flew low over the water, startling the fish who darted left to get away from her. When they did, Luna dove. Grabbing one fish with her sharp teeth, she tossed it to Estrid. The little fire dragon blew a ball of flame at the fish, charring it, then caught it before it fell. Then Luna and Wink both swooped low and snagged their own meals from the water. Happy with their catches, they sat on the stones to enjoy their fish.

"Good girls," I called to them. They clicked and chirped to one another and me. Their sounds resonated within me, a language mine but not mine.

When they were almost done, I climbed back to my feet once more. The girls chewed their last bites, one eye on me and one eye on the remains of their fish. They watched and waited. When I was sure they were finished eating, I turned and ran back inside once more. I took the long way, climbing up toward the top of the cave then back down a narrow passage, zigzagging across my own path to throw them off and see how good their sense of smell really was. Then, running, I sped back to the main living quarters.

Through the curtain of ivy and roots, I saw lightning strike in the distance. Rain pattered on the stone floor inside the cave, washing it with water. Breathless, I waited to see who would find me first.

It was Wink.

The air shivered, and the dragon appeared. She was truly the cleverest of all the sisters.

"Smartie." I pulled a biscuit from the jar and tossed it to her.

Luna and Estrid appeared a moment later.

Luna, whose face was covered in cobwebs, landed on the corner of the table and brushed the webs off her face. I was just on my way to help her when she let out the daintiest of sneezes.

A small flicker of blue light flew from the dragon's mouth. In the wake of the dragon fire, a small pile of moonstones lay on the table.

"My goodness, look at these," I said, lifting the pale blue stones. Like the sky on a cloudy morning, they were a mix of hazy white and hues of pale blue.

Luna purred proudly.

I patted her on the head. "Well done! We'll keep them somewhere special."

I slid the moonstones into my pocket. As Luna grew larger, her magical stones were also increasing in size and brilliance. I'd never forget the first tiny stone, no larger than a kernel of corn.

I was just headed to the biscuit jar to grabs snacks for Estrid and Luna when I heard a strange noise outside. At first, I thought it was a rumble of thunder, but then it sounded again. It was a strange trumpeting sound paired with odd clicks.

The dragons, who'd been fluttering about me happily in anticipation of another treat, turned and looked toward the cave opening.

"No," I whispered in a harsh warning, motioning for them to stay back.

The noise sounded once more. This time I heard it more distinctly over the rain. It was the blast of a horn, but there was something else, an odd scratching sound. And I heard clicks and beeps. The noise made a lump rise in my throat.

All three dragons moved toward the cave entrance.

"No. Stay back," I whispered.

Estrid and Luna, sensing my nervousness, flew back to me. Estrid perched on my shoulder; Luna clung to my long braid.

Wink, however, hovered closer to the cave entrance.

"Wink, don't you dare. Mother told us not to go outside. Please. It's not safe. Please, don't make me put you in the cage," I said, referring to the enchanted silver cage Mother had once brought. It was the only thing that could hold Wink and dispel her magic. I hated it. And so did Wink.

The dragon, who understood me very well, looked over her shoulder at me.

"Wink. No. Please."

Again the horn sounded.

My stomach quaked.

Wink looked back once more, and then she winked and disappeared.

3
NOT QUITE CAMELOT

I GASPED.

"Wink," I whispered.

My hands shaking, I approached the curtain of ivy.

Estrid and Luna flew toward the back of the cave. I swallowed hard then edged carefully over the wet stones to the ledge. Shifting a little of the vines out of the way, I looked outside.

Flying just off the coast was a small airship. A light mounted to the side of the ship scanned the seawall. I gazed at the sky overhead. It was dark, the moon hidden by the clouds. I couldn't see Wink. That was good news. If I couldn't see her, then no one else could either.

I looked back at the airship. It wasn't too far down the coast from me.

Lightning cracked.

When it did, I caught Wink's silhouette on the skyline. She was hovering above the ship.

"Wink," I whispered desperately.

The spotlight scanned down the seawall and into my cave. Bright light blasted into my eyes. The cave behind me was bathed in light. A sharp wind blew, shaking the ivy. Wincing, I looked away. The light glowed on the zoetrope, and the wind turned the delicate paper. Silhouettes of dragons flew along the walls as the zoetrope cast its shadows.

Once more, the strange machine sounded, echoing oddly, a mix of sounds like something metallic scraping, clicking, and beeping, paired with the trumpet of a horn. My stomach shook. I felt ill. My knees softened. In the back of the cave, Estrid and Luna chirped nervously.

I closed my eyes and prayed for the airship to pass, prayed for Wink to come back. I heard the sound of men's voices. The light faded. I listened to the purring sound of the airship as it flew further down the coast and away from my cave.

Hands shaking, I went to the telescope. Through it, I watched as the airship flew toward the village, scanning the seawall as it went. I gazed down at the shoreline. The beach was completely covered with water. The storm had eroded any sign of safe passage to my cave. I was safe here. There was no way they would ever suspect anything or anyone was living in here. Everything was going to be okay. No one had seen Wink or me.

Blasted dragon.

Sitting down on the wet stones, I gathered all my hair and set it in my lap. I inhaled then exhaled deeply. I couldn't hear the airship anymore. It was gone. It was safe now.

Closing my eyes, I bent my thoughts toward Wink, and then I sang:

From Avalon to Camelot
Sir Pellinore did ride
With Arthur there
Excalibur strapped along his side
The Questing Beast they hunted long
Searching night and day
But t'was the love of Gwenhwyfar

Whose call he could not fight
For Camelot
For Avalon
For these, I do implore
My sweet dear one
I call you now
Come back upon my shore

I exhaled deeply and opened my eyes. Spinning all around me was a torrent of shimmering blue light. Estrid and Luna, lulled by the song, perched on the back of the kitchen chairs and watched me. Dragon caller. That was what Mother had called me. That was why the dragons had awakened from their long slumber. They'd heard my song and woke.

A moment later, the air shimmered, and Wink appeared once more.

I sighed with relief then rose.

"Bad girl," I chided her. "You could have been seen."

Wink snorted a perturbed huff at me.

"Mother said we should not go out. That sound… You all felt it too, right?" I asked, looking at all three of them. Luna and Estrid watched me with curiosity. "It wasn't safe. Mother warned me that we should stay inside."

Ignoring me, Wink flew to the back of the cave.

Annoyed, I pinned up my long hair and followed her. Estrid and Luna followed me, curious to see the outcome of this battle.

"Wink! Wink, come back here," I called, but the stubborn dragon flew on.

I wound through the caves, following behind Wink. Bending low, I shimmied into the narrow shaft through which Wink had gone. We were deep underground now. Here, the air smelled of minerals and clay. Following Wink, I entered the massive interior chamber at the very back of the cave. The cavern, trimmed with amethysts, sparkled. A small oil lamp, which we kept perpetually lit, cast its glow around the room. I scanned the chamber for Wink, furious with her for putting us all at risk.

But my heart melted when I saw her.

Her sisters flew in behind me then joined her. The three of them nestled inside a cracked geode at the other end of the cave. There, they snuggled around the last unhatched dragon egg. The pearlescent egg, looking like a smooth quartz crystal, twinkled in the dim light.

Suddenly feeling sorry for having scolded her, I joined them. The geode was large enough to house them, but not me. Sitting beside the stone, I set my chin on my hands and looked at them.

Wink gave me a passing glance, a half-apology in her eyes, then set her head on the unhatched egg. No. I couldn't be angry at her. I could barely stand this semi-prison myself. I couldn't blame her for being curious.

I sighed. "Still won't wake up, huh?" I asked the egg.

The others looked at me expectantly.

Dragon caller. I had woken all three sisters with my songs. The eggs, stashed here hundreds of years ago by Merlin, had been waiting for someone to wake them. I'd sung to each of the girls, waking them from their long slumber, but the fourth egg wouldn't stir—no matter what song I warbled. The dragon inside was still alive. When I put my ear to the egg, I could hear its heart beating. But no matter how much I called, no matter what song I sang—and I'd sung them all, made up new ones, sung in Latin, French, and even Seelie, the strange language Mother had taught me—the dragon would not wake.

"One day, I will find the right song."

After all, if I couldn't do it, who would? How many hundreds of years would have to pass? Legend said that every nine generations, a dragon caller would be born. And that was me. There hadn't been another since the time of King Arthur.

That's what Mother told me. Well, I called her Mother, but she was not my true parent. Gothel had raised, loved, mothered, and protected me. She was my guardian. But she was not really my mother. She was a faerie sworn to protect the line of Pendragon. Every nine generations, the old blood, the blood of dragon would awaken. Pendragon. That was me, a descendant of King Arthur, Rapunzel Pendragon, cave-dwelling heir of Camelot.

4
ET TU, MISTER DARCY?

I STAYED WITH THE DRAGONS UNTIL THEY FELL ASLEEP. WITH the momentary excitement passed, I went back to the front of the cave. Sliding carefully on the wet cave floor near the entrance, I peered outside. The rain had stopped, and the clouds had moved off. The sky was filled with thousands of stars. Pushing the ivy aside, I scanned up and down the shoreline. There was no sign of the airship.

There was no way anyone on that ship had seen me. The massive oak tree that grew on the land overhead and its long, thick roots, entwined with the cascade of ivy, kept the entrance to this ancient cave secret. No one would have seen.

What was that strange noise? The odd sound had tugged at something inside me. Was this what Mother was worried about? Was someone looking for me?

No. That wasn't possible. No one even knew I was alive save Mother.

I was no one. A hobgoblin in a cave. Not one of *the young ladies* at all. No matter how nice that would be, how normal, that wasn't me. I was a girl in a cave with three tiny dragons and a dragon egg to look after. They were my treasure, and I was destined to stay here and guard them.

Forever.

Sighing, I grabbed my copy of Miss Austen's book, stoked the fire, and put on a fresh pot of tea. I lit a single candle then sat down at the table, dumping my hair beside me. It felt good to get its weight off my head. Sometimes I wanted to cut it all off—and once, I had. But it just regrew within days, a peculiarity I didn't understand and for which Mother had no reasonable explanation either.

I flipped to the chapter where I'd left off. Certainly, Jane Austen's character, Miss Elizabeth Bennet, didn't have such trouble with her hair. We did, however, both have fine eyes. Perhaps if I ever found my Mister Darcy, he'd like my kaleidoscope eyes. After I read a few more chapters, I went and poured myself a cup of tea. When I returned to the table, I eyed the zoetrope sitting there, remembering the momentary flash of the dragons on the wall as the airship had passed.

I gazed out toward the cave entrance again. Thunder rumbled in the distance, and there was a light rain falling again, but there was no sign of airships. Only the soft peal of my wind chime filled the air.

Lifting my candle, I lit the small taper at the center of the zoetrope and gave it a spin.

A moment later, dragons danced across the wall. They breathed fire as they flew through the illusory sky. The dragons' silhouettes spun around the room, interrupted only by my shadow. I turned it again and again, giggling happily as I watched the beautiful design at work.

I would need to show the girls. Setting my bookmark in my book once more, I took a quick sip of my tea, placing the cup down too quickly in the saucer. The china clattered.

"Oops," I said with a laugh then to headed toward the back of the cave, but then I heard a bizarre noise. A sound like something metal zipping quickly buzzed just outside the cave. There was an odd clunk in the rocks and then the sound of a machine working.

I rose. Gripping the back of the chair, I stared at the cave entrance.

Sensing my alarm, Estrid suddenly appeared. She blew out the candles I had lit then alighted on my shoulder.

A moment later, the ivy parted, and a hand appeared on the cave floor.

First a hand.

Then a shoulder.

Then a leg.

And then a man.

For a moment, I'd stopped breathing.

He pulled himself into the cave then stood.

Green light glowed from the goggles he wore. He pulled a small device from his belt and activated it. It clicked loudly.

He scanned the room with his strange machine.

Estrid snarled low and mean.

I gripped the back of the chair tightly. I felt fixed, frozen in place. Part of me told me to lift the chair and bash him over the head with it. The other part of me—which had never even seen a man in the flesh before—stared in disbelief.

When the stranger finally set his eyes on me, he stopped. He pushed his goggles back on top of his head and looked at me, his eyes wide. He lifted his device and pointed it at me. Lights flashed across the top of the small machine, and it clicked wildly.

"You?" he whispered.

And then he did what he shouldn't have.

He stepped toward me.

Estrid, having decided that was enough, crawled out of her hiding place behind my long braid and flew between us.

Flames flickered between her jaws, and a moment later, she blasted a fireball at the stranger.

"Look out," I called.

The man jumped back, his device falling to the floor with a clatter as it smashed into a dozen pieces.

The man slipped on the wet cave floor. His feet went out from under him, and he slid toward the ledge. I gasped in horror. If he fell, he would surely die. He grabbed at the ivy, but it pulled away in handfuls. Desperate, he reached out and held on to the wet ledge. I watched in terror as his fingers slowly slipped.

Rushing to the ledge, I reached out for him.

"Take my hands," I called.

The stranger grabbed for me, his hands in mine. Tugging with all my might, I slowly pulled him back up. Once he was safely inside, I jumped backed, edging toward the table. I could run. There were many places to hide in the cave. But first and foremost, I had to get to the egg.

Estrid landed on my shoulder and roared more loudly than I thought possible. Her teeth bared.

The man rose quickly. He stared from me to Estrid.

A moment later, Wink appeared, Luna right behind her.

The man lifted his finger and whispered under his breath, "one, two, three," as he counted each of the dragons. Then he pointed to me.

"Pendragon," he said.

Wink, who apparently had had enough of the intruder, blinked. Reappearing before the man, she exhaled a puff of pink smoke in his face.

The stranger's eyes rolled back, and he crumpled to the floor.

5
WWEBD?

WRINGING MY HANDS, I PACED THE CAVE. CASTING A GLANCE down at the man who lay unconscious on the floor, I stopped. His shirt was wet. His sleeves, which had been rolled up, showed his arms which were covered in gooseflesh. He was cold. Grabbing a quilt from the cupboard, I covered him. He didn't move. Pausing, I bent down to have a look. He had dark, curly hair. He was probably the same age as me. And he was handsome. Very handsome. A very handsome someone who'd likely come to kill me. Wonderful.

I rose and paced again.

What to do? What to do?

"What would Mother do?" I mused aloud.

Mother would have Estrid fry him to a crisp then toss him into the sea.

Okay, not that. Fine. Well then, what would Elizabeth Bennet do?

I shook my head. I hadn't finished the book yet. I only got to the part where Lady Catherine de Bourgh confronted Elizabeth in the garden. Ugh. I didn't know what to do. Should I bat my fine eyes and say something witty? I wrung my hands.

With the water so high, I couldn't leave the cave now even if I wanted to. And if I did, what about my girls? I could throw him out of the cave, but he'd drown, and I'd just saved him from drowning. And even if I did get him out of the cave, now he knew I was here, the cave was here, and he'd seen the girls. I could tie him up. That might work. I could bash him on the head with a frying pan, but that would just give him brain damage and very likely kill him. What to do!

I went to the telescope. Scanning, I spotted a boat moored at the base of the seawall just below my home.

I turned to pace once more, then spotted the stranger's broken device lying on the floor. Metal gears, coils, and glass were scattered all around. I scooped up the pieces and went to go grab the dustpan when I spotted something shimmering in the moonlight. Lying just inside the broken contraption was a metal shard that looked like the amulet Mother wore. It was mounted inside the device, wires attached to the slim, jagged piece of metal. I picked up the broken instrument and pried the piece out, holding it in the palm of my hand.

To my surprise, the metal shimmered blue the same way Mother's did when I touched it. It was similar, but not the same piece of metal.

I slipped the metal piece into my pocket then bent to cleaned up the mess. Wink and Estrid perched on the backs of the dining table chairs like vultures, each of them observing the stranger carefully. Luna, feeling more shy, clung to my hair, looking but not wanting to get too far from me.

Once the mess was cleaned up, I studied the man once more.

He wore a leather jacket on which he had a lapel pin. It appeared to be a badge of some kind. A brisk wind blew in through the cave entrance. The man shuddered in his sleep.

I looked back at Wink. "And how long should we expect our guest to be unconscious?"

She snorted at me then turned back to watch the stranger once more.

I eyed the man again. I needed to get him off the wet floor. Right now, I wasn't sure if I needed to kill him or keep him from catching a cold. I had no idea who he was, but he had known who I was. On the one hand, maybe that meant Mother had sent him. On the other hand, chances were also good that he was there to kill me.

Odds were fifty-fifty.

Well, no, more like a seventy-thirty. It was far more likely that he was there to kill me, yet he didn't look much like a killer.

A soft breeze blew through the cave, fluttering a curl on his forehead.

No, he didn't look like a killer at all.

Still warring with myself, I rose and removed the blanket, setting it at the foot of the small lounging couch we'd arranged along the cave wall.

"All right, sir." I slipped my hands under his armpits and tugged him toward the chaise. "I'm not sure if you're here to help me or murder me, but all the same, let's get you off the floor."

Estrid flew to the ledge just above the couch. Orange flame flickered in her mouth as she watched the man carefully. I lifted his shoulders first. Getting him onto the chaise wasn't easy. Boosting the rest of him up with my hip and leg, I rolled him onto the divan. He lay at an awkward and very uncomfortable angle, but still, he didn't wake.

I looked back at Wink. "Whatever that butterfly dragon fire of yours is, promise me you will never use it on me."

Wink chirped at me then eyed the man suspiciously once more.

I adjusted the gentleman into a comfortable position, feeling awkward the entire time considering I had never even seen a man up close before, let alone touched one. When I was done, I covered him again.

"There," I said, clapping my hands off. I gazed down at him. His dark hair, on closer inspection, and under the light of Estrid's ominous fireball of death, was really more amber colored. The color reminded me of a chocolate bar Mother had once brought me. He had a sprinkle of freckles on his nose and cheeks.

I frowned. He definitely didn't look like a killer.

I eyed the silver badge on his jacket once more.

"Watch him," I whispered to Estrid. The dragon shifted forward and glared down at him.

Moving gingerly, I unpinned the badge. The image thereon was vaguely familiar. My mind raced through the pages of my books until I recalled where I had seen the symbol before.

I rushed back to my library. I pulled a tome from the shelf then headed back into the central living space. Slipping into a chair at the table from which I could keep an eye on the stranger, I flipped through the pages of the book.

I laid the silver badge on the table then opened my tome of Arthurian tales, flipping to an illustration that was included with the tales of King Pellinore. On the king's shield was the grail. Wrapped around the cup was the Questing Beast, the dragon King Pellinore always hunted—but never managed to slay. I looked at the stranger's badge. There were some small differences between King Pellinore's crest and the badge. The letters R and M had been worked into the stranger's brooch. But there was one other importance difference. While King Pellinore's sigil only showed the Questing Beast and the grail together, the stranger's badge had a unique addition. On his sigil, the Questing Beast had a sword thrust through its neck.

I set the pin down and stared at the man.

I knew then what he was. For all his sweet appearance,

there was a sad but simple truth. This man was a dragon hunter.

I turned to Wink.

"We're in trouble. Find Mother."

The little dragon chirped and, with a shiver of magic, disappeared.

6
PETTICOATS
AND PENDRAGONS

I BREWED A FRESH POT OF TEA AND SAT IN A CHAIR OPPOSITE the stranger. Estrid kept one eye on the man while she dozed. Luna had taken up a more cautious position inside an unused teapot on the shelf opposite. I sipped my tea as I rolled the piece of metal that had been in the man's device around in my hand. It was exactly like Mother's. How had he come by it? For that matter, what even was it? And why did it glow blue every time I touched it?

Lifting my teacup, I took a sip. I gazed toward the cave entrance. It was that hazy gray color it gets right before the sun rises. Wink wasn't back yet. My stomach tied into a knot. Had I endangered her as well by sending her to get help?

I set down my cup and lined up the various weapons I had lying on the table beside me: a fire iron, a butcher knife, a cast iron pan, and my pointiest hairpin.

I examined the sliver of metal. It didn't really have any definitive shape. I looked it over, searching for any markings, but there were none.

Frowning, I set it back down. Miss Austen's book sat on the

table. It called to me, tantalizing me with its unanswered secrets. Would Mister Darcy return? Would Elizabeth realize she was in love with him? Would they both stop being so stubborn?

I looked away from the book. It would have to wait. I picked up the mysterious shard once more.

"It's a piece of metal."

I turned to see the man staring at me. He hadn't moved at all. In fact, he looked far too comfortable lying there under my quilt, his head on my pillow. He had a soft, friendly expression on his face. Despite his kind appearance, his badge told a far different tale.

"I know it's a piece of metal," I said.

He cast a glance up at Estrid, who was watching him carefully. She, in turn, cast a glance at me: *fireball him or no,* her eyes asked.

I shook my head.

The stranger watched our exchange. "Okay if I sit up?" he asked.

"Sit up, yes. Get up, no."

"Understood," he said then cast a smile at Estrid who glared menacingly at him. He flexed his eyebrows in surprise then shook his head. "I don't suppose I could have some water? I have an odd taste in my mouth." He sucked in his lips and gave his head a shake. "Probably the dragon breath."

"It wasn't her breath. It was butterfly dragon fire," I said. "Water or tea?"

"A spot of tea would be lovely."

"When I get up, don't try anything stupid or Estrid will roast you for dinner. Understood?"

"Understood. Message loud and clear, Estrid," he said, saluting my little dragon who flattened her ears at the sound of a stranger using her name. She puffed a little cloud of fire at him. The stranger rubbed the back of his head. "I see. Not on a first name basis yet. Got it."

I went to the fireplace and lifted the teapot. Pulling down a cup and saucer, I poured the man some tea.

"How about you? You have a name?" the stranger asked me.

"Not one that you need to know," I replied tartly. I envisioned Elizabeth Bennet grinning approvingly at me. "And you, Mister Dragon Hunter? A name?"

"Dragon hunter is a bit of a misnomer. Ewan...Ewan Goodwin."

"Tea or honey, Mister Goodwin?"

"Neither."

Willing my hands to stay still, I carried the cup of tea to him. As I approached, I saw him look me over. Good lord, I hadn't even thought to put any clothes on. There I was in a corset and petticoat serving tea to a man who had probably come to kill me. Looking respectfully away from my mostly underdressed form, his gaze went to my hair and then to my eyes. He stared at my eyes, his gaze lingering far too long.

The teacup in my hand started to rattle.

"Here you are, Mister Goodwin," I said politely, handing him the cup.

"Thank you." He took the cup, his dark brown eyes still fixed on mine.

I went to the other side of the room and lifted a shawl hanging on a peg in the cave wall. I draped it over my shoulders, covering my bare arms and chest. My stomach twisted with both fear and embarrassment. If Mother were here, she could merely tap my gown and shift it into something proper. Me, well, a shawl and my hair would have to do.

I pushed my long braid over my shoulder and down my chest then went and sat opposite the stranger once more.

"So, Mister Goodwin," I began, picking up my teacup. "Have you come to kill me?"

"Well—" He lifted his finger while he took a sip. "Good tea. Thank you again. Well, *you* aren't quite what I was expecting to find. And I wasn't expecting *them* at all," he said, looking from Estrid to Luna. "Where is the third one? The one with the bad breath?"

I frowned at him. "That was butterfly dragon fire. I told you that already. Never mind where she is. And now?"

"Now what?"

"And now, are you going to kill me?"

"And now, you are a pretty young lady all by yourself, not a dragon-blooded thug. Also, I have no idea what to do about the actual dragons since, you know, they aren't supposed to exist. Besides, I'm rather certain Estrid will roast me alive if I even look at you sideways, so…"

I lifted the brooch he'd been wearing. "What's this?"

"That," he said, glancing down at his chest then back, "is my badge. Did you take it off me?"

"But what *is* it?"

He sipped again. "I am a member of the Red Cape Society, a special branch of Her Majesty's secret service. I'm a Pellinore, and that's my badge."

"A Pellinore."

"Exactly."

"Like King Pellinore? The Knight of the Questing Beast? Otherwise known as a dragon hunter?" I asked, tapping his badge.

"Well, sort of."

"Do you hunt dragons?"

"I hunt dragon bloods."

"Dragon bloods?"

"You know, the blood of the dragon—I mean, of course,

they don't actually shift into dragons, but they carry the blood of Pendragon, which gives them extra-human strength, fiery red eyes, occasionally a little firepower from the fingers— always getting themselves in trouble with the law. Generally thugs and bruisers, not a dainty thing like you. I was tracking one through Cornwall, followed him to a carriage station not far from here, a big lug who is always up to no good. No idea what he was doing this far away from London, but I suspected he was planning something awful, so I was following him. But my machine," he said, motioning to the broken device lying on the table, "went mad and led me to you instead. Of course, I've never seen a female dragon blood before. You aren't supposed to exist. Unless... Well, that's impossible. So, yeah. That's my story. I came here to arrest a dragon blood and instead, I found you and this cute—but very deadly—little brood instead. And that catches us up to now. And your name again?"

"Never said."

"Right. So, I see that shard glows blue when you touch it."

"The metal," I said, picking it up again.

"Yes. The metal."

"This metal powered your device? It led you to me?"

"Indeed it did."

"Are there more machines like this?"

"Um, no. That one *was* special. Irreplaceable, in fact. So there's that."

"And this...metal. Are there other pieces of metal like this?"

"Also no."

"Then why do you have it?"

"That's complicated."

"Okay," I said then rolled the metal around in my hand once more. "What is it?"

"Metal. I think we have already established that."

"Right. But it's not just any metal, is it?"

"Also complicated."

I frowned then looked up at him. "My name is Rapunzel… Rapunzel Pendragon."

"The metal is a shard from the sword Excalibur, enchanted by Merlin, and bound to the blood of Pendragon. In other words, to you."

7
PROMISES, PROMISES

I TAPPED MY FINGERS ON THE BOOK SITTING ON THE TABLE as I ruminated on his words. There were others out there like me. Others who carried the Pendragon line. Why hadn't Mother ever told me that?

"The dragon bloods you mentioned...you said they have powers?" I asked.

"Yes. And not ones they generally use for good."

I looked up at Estrid. Were the other dragon callers like me? Maybe not the evil men this dragon hunter was mentioning, but others? Maybe there was someone who could wake the other dragon egg. "And you've never seen one of them before?" I asked, pointing to the dragons.

"No one has. They don't exist. Except, you know, the fact they are *right there*. Them and you."

"Me?"

"Right. A female Pendragon. I mean, you aren't supposed to exist either. The bloodline carries on, but only males exhibit the gifts from Mordred. Never the women. But your eyes...remarkable."

Mordred? I frowned.

A moment later, the air shivered, and Wink reappeared. She paused a moment to shake the rain off her wings then looked from me to Ewan. She opened her snout and began heaving another breath of pink air.

"No. Wait," I called to her.

Confused, the dragon flew back to me, alighting on my shoulder. I set my hand on her head.

"You're cold and wet," I told her, pulling off my shawl and wrapping it gently around her wings. "Did you find her?"

The dragon clicked affirmatively.

"Is she coming?"

More clicks.

Holding the dragon against me, I rose. "Well, now we have a problem," I told Ewan.

"How so?"

"Well, maybe you didn't come here to kill me, but someone is coming who will most definitely kill you."

At that, he stood.

Estrid readied her flame ball, but I motioned for her to wait.

"No getting up, remember?" I told him.

"I remember, but whoever is coming... That's a problem. I'm a man of the law, not a ruffian or thief. I'm not going to sit idly by and wait for someone to come murder me," he said then dipped into his vest, pulling out—albeit slowly—a pistol. "Easy," he told Estrid, holding the weapon loosely in one hand, raising the other in surrender. "Look, if I wanted to do anything, I could have. Rule number one of holding a prisoner: always check them for weapons."

"Well, you're my first."

Ewan smirked. The expression on his face, and the fact my witty comeback made him smile, brought a blush to my cheeks.

"Okay," he said, slipping the pistol back into his vest. "May I make a proposal?"

"I'm listening."

"I leave," he said, pointing to the cave entrance. "Forget I ever saw you. Forget about this place and your unusual *pets*. And you," he said, pointing to me, "let me go before whatever bad thing on its way arrives."

"How do I know you won't tell anyone about us?"

"Well, first, no one in their right mind would believe me. And second, you have my word as a gentleman and as an agent of Her Majesty's Red Cape Society—Pellinore Division."

I looked at him. He had such an earnest expression on his face. In truth, I didn't know what to do. He could return here with a battalion of soldiers and take me and my dragons prisoner. After all, he'd already told me he tracked my kind. Well, not my kind exactly, but others with blood like me.

"I can see you're thinking it over. Prudence. That's good. Don't just trust anyone. But you have my word," Ewan said.

"What's your word to me? I know nothing about you."

"Rapunzel, you might be a dragon blood, but you are nothing like the others I've seen. You are a true Pendragon. You carry the blood of our Once and Future King. And for the first time in my life, I see in you what the old stories always whispered to be true. The royal blood of Arthur lives on. Pellinores hunt their Questing Beasts, but we are also loyal to the King of Camelot...and his true heirs. You have my word."

My stomach shook. Mother would be here soon. I had to do something. "Your word," I whispered.

"My word."

"You will never come back here. And you will never tell anyone about me."

"I promise."

"Then go," I said, tilting my head toward the cave entrance.

He rose, casting a careful glance at Estrid, then came close to me. Close up, I could see his eyes were not just brown but were the color of honey, a warm gold and chestnut combination. My stomach quaked.

"Can I have that?" he asked, pointing to his badge.

I shook my head. "No. That's mine. Dragons horde treasure, remember? Just be glad I'm letting *you* leave."

"Are you calling me a treasure?"

I smirked. "Just go."

"What about that?" he asked, pointing to the fragment of Excalibur.

"Definitely not."

"Okay. I'll go, but I don't fly well. Have a ladder?"

Setting Wink down, I went to the cave entrance. I unpinned my long locks. I then wound my braid around the hook in the wall and motioned to him.

"Okay. That's different. Doesn't it hurt?"

"Not at all. Goodbye, Ewan."

Gently grabbing my braid, he nodded to me once more then began to lower himself from the cave. I watched as he rappelled down the face of the seawall. The tide below had receded just a little, allowing him to get to his waiting boat more easily. I cast a glance out at the water. The gray of dawn had faded, and the first rosy glows of the sunrise shimmered on the horizon. When he was finally on the beach, I began pulling my long braid back up. Wading out to his boat, he climbed inside and began to row. Standing at the entrance to the cave, I watched him go. He was a good distance away when he called out to me.

"Rapunzel?"

Holding onto the hook I used for my hair, I pushed the ivy aside and leaned out to see better.

"Rule number two of keeping prisoners: always watch for

sleight of hand. Sorry," he called with a wave then went back to rowing once more.

Scowling, I turned and went back inside. Sitting on the table were the broken pieces of his device and his badge, but the shard of Excalibur was gone.

8
MOTHER KNOWS BEST, RIGHT?

I SCANNED THE ROOM, LOOKING AT THE DRAGONS WHO WERE all staring at me. What in the world had just happened? Had I made the right choice? What was Mother going to say? And more importantly, what was she going to do?

Pacing the room nervously, I decided that in the end, it was already done. Whatever happened now would happen. It wasn't my fault he had found me. It was the device he had. Somehow, it had led him to me. And he said there weren't any more like it. And he had promised he wouldn't tell anyone about me. He would keep his promise, wouldn't he?

Feeling fidgety, I took the teacups to the bin and washed them. I then went back to the couch and folded up the blanket with which I had covered him. I lifted the fabric to my nose. There was the familiar smell of the beach and the wind, but under that, I caught the unfamiliar scents of lemon and lavender mixed with a musky scent—his smell. I inhaled deeply then folded the blanket back up.

"Really, Rapunzel. Don't get romantic. No one falls in love with a man they just met. Especially not one who potentially wanted to kill them," I chided myself aloud.

At that, Estrid snorted in agreement.

"Exactly." But as I folded, I kept thinking about those warm eyes and chocolate-colored curls.

Shaking myself from my thoughts, I finished tidying up then sat back down. Wink yawned tiredly. All the excitement done, she and Estrid flew to the back of the cave where they slept. Luna had fallen asleep in the teapot on the shelf.

I sat at the table turning the badge around and around with my finger.

There were others like me.

There were others like me, but they were dangerous creatures.

I cast a glance at the entrance of the cave. Mother would come soon. Once Mother arrived, everything would become clear. Everything would be all right. Mother always knew the best thing to do. Mother would keep me safe.

Picking up Miss Austen's book, I flipped to the chapter where I'd left off. Part of me hoped Elizabeth married Darcy just to spite Lady Catherine de Bourgh, to rebel, to be free. But first, she had to heal her own prejudiced heart. Or was it pride? Clever, Miss Austen. They were both pride and prejudice. And if they were ever going to fall in love properly, they would need to overcome them both.

An image of Ewan flashed through my mind once more.

Clearing my throat, I forced the image away and settled in with Mister Darcy once again.

As the final wedding bell tolled on the double wedding of Mister Bingley to Jane Bennet and Mister Darcy to Elizabeth Bennet—my victorious heroine—my eyes began to droop. I finished the last words on the page then closed the book and set my head down on the delicious tome. Scanning the table, my eyes rested on Ewan's badge. I wrapped my hand around the small piece then slowly drifted off to sleep.

It must have been late in the afternoon when I heard a familiar voice call my name.

"Rapunzel? Rapunzel, are you there? Rapunzel?" I woke groggily and went to the cave entrance.

"Mother?"

"Thank the gods. Are you all right?"

"Yes."

"Please let down your hair."

Hands shaking, I lowered my braid to the ground. At the sound of Mother's voice, all three dragons returned to the central living space.

I stared out at the water as Mother climbed up. The waves were a soft blue color. A breeze blew onto my face. I closed my eyes, relishing the feeling of the wind caressing my cheek. A moment later, Mother climbed into the room. She wrapped her arms around me at once, shifting from child to woman in one swift motion.

"Oh, Rapunzel. Thank goodness. When Wink appeared, I couldn't believe my eyes. I thought maybe you'd gotten ill or fallen. I couldn't discern from Wink what had happened. Thank goodness you're—" Her voice fell flat as she looked at the table. Wordlessly, she left me then went to investigate the pieces of the device that lay scattered there.

"Rapunzel?" she whispered.

I crossed the room and held out my hand. In my palm was the badge. She reached out to touch it, but her hand recoiled as the steel with which the badge was made burned her fingertips.

"What...what happened?" she asked, her dark eyes wide.

"Someone found me."

"Found you? What are you talking about?"

I reached out and touched the amulet she always wore. The

piece glowed blue at my touch. "He had a piece of metal just like yours. He coupled it with that device, and it led him to me. He said he used the device to find others like me."

Mother's eyes widened even further. "Another shard? That's impossible. Are you certain?"

I nodded. "Yes, I held it with my own hand. It...responded."

Mother looked at the badge. "Where is he?"

I bit the inside of my cheek. Truth or lie? Truth or lie? "I let him go."

The lines around Mother's mouth twitched. "You let him go?"

"He told me he is a man of the law. He hunts others like me who are...bad. He promised he wouldn't tell anyone about me."

"Do you know what that symbol is?" she asked, motioning to the badge.

"It is the crest of King Pellinore."

"Yes. King Pellinore, the dragon slayer, the hunter of the Questing Beast. This person who found you, he and others like him marshal this realm, impose rules on those of us who are... different. You made a terrible mistake. You cannot trust him. Did he see the girls?"

"Yes. Estrid almost roasted him alive."

"You should have let her. You are in great danger now, Rapunzel. All of you."

"How could I just kill an innocent man? Mother, you never told me there are others like me. How many others are there? Are there other dragon callers? Maybe someone else could wake the egg. We need to find the others. I shouldn't just stay here, hiding in this place like a hobgoblin if there are others out there like me."

"Those others.... They are not like you, Rapunzel. There is no one else like you."

"But Ewan said there are other dragon bloods, men with fierce blood who can—"

"Ewan?"

"The...dragon hunter."

Mother raised an eyebrow at me. Taking my hand, she sat me down. "There *are* others who carry the Pendragon blood, but they are not like you, my love."

"Why not? Mother, you must explain all this to me. Please, I am not a child anymore. And I am in danger. I need to know why, exactly."

Mother sighed. "Very well. You are the blood of Pendragon. You already know this. But how is more important. The most popular legends say that Arthur had only one child, Mordred, the son of an incestuous liaison between him and his half-sister Morgan. It is true that Mordred was his son and that Morgan was the child's mother. Morgan was turned by the Unseelie court and practiced their dark magic. Mordred's descendants live on. But their line is tainted by the influence of the Unseelie. The dragon bloods this Ewan told you about are the bloodline of Mordred.

"But Arthur had a wife, Gwenhwyfar. She was not a lover of Lancelot. She was not a dimwitted whore. Gwenhwyfar, the white phantom, was a practitioner of the old ways and much loved by the Seelie. From her union with Arthur, a daughter, Anna, was born."

"But all the stories say she was barren," I interjected.

"That is because they are stories. Take it from someone who remembers."

"You were there?"

Mother smiled sadly. "Yes. Anna survived the fall of Camelot, but she was hunted by Mordred's heirs. With our help, she disappeared, carrying with her the true blood of Pendragon. Anna was born of the Once and Future King and Gwenhwyfar, the white phantom. You are the last surviving descendant of that line. It is Anna's blood you carry. And that is the reason I am here, to protect you as I once did Anna."

I stared at Mother. "What you're saying is…"

"Truth. This hunter you met, are you certain—are you *very* certain—that he had a metal shard like mine?"

"He said it was a shard from the sword Excalibur. He was hunting another dragon blood when the shard led him here instead. Is it true? Is this really a shard of Excalibur?"

"Yes." Mother began pacing the room.

"Why doesn't the shard burn you?" I asked. Steel always burned mother's hands, but not the small amulet she wore.

"It is made of star metal and bound to the blood of Pendragon," she said absently as she continued pacing. She passed the table once more, stopping to look at the metal device. "He took the shard with him?"

"Yes. I tried to stop him, but… He tricked me," I said, unable to hide the quick smile that lit up my face. Clever man. I cast a glance at Mother, relieved to see she had not seen me smile. I smothered my expression.

"And he said there was another dragon blood near here?"

"In Cornwall. Ewan had been tracking him."

Mother frowned hard. "Mordred's heirs are hunting you. You're not safe here. As it was, all signs were leading to danger. That is why I went to see my people. You are not safe even in Merlin's cave."

"But…why? Why are the other dragon bloods hunting me?"

"Because they will take you, your womb, your dragons, and your blood to use as their own. If the bloodlines ever combine… It would be catastrophic. They would use you to reclaim this realm at the bidding of the Unseelie Queen. Rapunzel, we must leave this place. It isn't safe."

"But what about the dragons?"

Mother smiled gently. She reached out to pet Wink. When

her fingers touched the tiny dragon, Wink transformed into a tabby cat. "What dragons?"

Wink spun in circles looking at herself. She then winked, appearing in the air nearby, only to fall—landing on her feet—to the floor. Wink flicked her tail and glared with annoyance at Mother.

"But everything I have is here," I whispered. "And the other egg."

Mother nodded. "We will have to take it with us."

I looked around the cave. So, my life was in danger. I could potentially be kidnapped, raped, and murdered. I was being hunted. But, for the first time ever, I would be able to leave the cave. See some place new. It was everything I'd ever wanted, under the worst possible conditions.

I picked up the copy of Miss Austen's book and smiled at Mother. "I'll get my things."

9
SHE'S GOT BIG DREAMS

Two cases and one bag. That was all we could afford to take with us. A lifetime's worth of blankets, cups, books—I mostly felt bad about the books—and accumulated nothings sat forgotten in the cave.

I scrunched the sand between my toes. Taking a deep breath, I waded into the surf, enjoying the sensation of the foamy bubbles tickling my ankles. Closing my eyes, I looked up at the sky, feeling the sun kiss my cheeks and warm my hair. In a crate sitting on the sand not far from me, the "cats" meowed loudly, wanting to come join the fun.

Turning back, I went to them. I knelt down in the sand and looked inside at the three miserable little dragons who definitely didn't want to be cats.

"When we get wherever we are going, I promise you, I'll let you out. I don't know where we're going myself. And right now, all of us are in danger. I'm sorry," I whispered.

Luna meowed nervously.

I cast a glance at Mother. She was standing on the beach with her arms raised. I watched as she worked. Silver sparkles danced from her fingers toward the cliff wall. The ivy and tree roots that used to drape over the opening of the cave grew thick. The roots widened and expanded so much that there was no way to even pass through. Now that it was completely hidden behind the roots and vines, no one would ever even know the cave entrance was there.

When she was done, Mother nodded. Digging in her bag, she handed me some stockings and a pair of boots. I slipped them on. As I did so, Mother tapped her fingers against her body, and a moment later, she shifted into the form of a hulking man. She towered over me in height and appeared to be a wall of muscle. She was tall, bald, and had a mean expression. But she also wore a fine suit and top hat.

Mother gave me an assessing look then reached out and touched the hem of my petticoat. A moment later, my gown shifted into a light purple-colored dress. It was a pretty, feminine thing with silk ribbons on the bodice and lace on the trim. Looking down at the garment, I wrinkled my nose.

"No?" Mother asked.

I giggled to hear her deep, masculine voice.

I shook my head. "Too prissy. I was thinking…maybe trousers and a leather bodice. You know, in the style of some of the more sporting ladies—airship jockeys, steamcar drivers, and the like."

"I see," Mother said, an amused expression playing on her —his—lips.

She twitched her fingers, and once more my garments transformed. This time, I found myself clad in trousers, a leather bodice with a soft white shirt underneath, and a mini top hat on my head. I wiggled my fingers, on which I wore fingerless gloves. Perfection. I pinned up my hair into a massive braid. It didn't look half bad.

"Thank you," I said then grinned at Mother. "Not planning to sport a moustache?"

She shook her head. "Not the fashion. And itchy. Let's go,"

she said then picked up the two cases, leaving the bag in which I'd packed the egg for me to carry. The little dragon egg was hard as stone, but I had still wrapped it up as best I could. Carrying my precious cargo, Mother hauling the crate with the girls, I followed behind her as we made our way down the beach.

Walking on sand was not as easy and carefree as I'd always thought it would be. About an hour into the walk, my feet started to hurt and sweat trickled down my back, but I would never complain. This was what it felt like to live. This was what it felt like to be free. Who could complain about that?

It took almost another hour before Mother motioned to me that we should turn off the beach. Winding through a narrow passage of rocks, we found our way to the top of the cliff. I was amazed to see the bright green field stretch out before me. My heart thundered in my chest. All this time, I had lived below a field full of purple asters, yellow-eyed daises, and ruby-colored poppies.

We headed out across the field. The smell of the grass, and the flowers effervescing in the bright sunlight, filled my senses. Holding out my hand, I let my palms touch the tips of the grass. It was strange how I could feel them but also so much more. I could feel the land under my hands. I could feel the earth. As I walked, I closed my eyes. When I did so, I heard whispers. A soft voice sang just outside of my hearing. I could only pick out a single line:

I've been the shadow in the cave.

I stopped.

Mother looked back at me, her eyes drifting from my face to my outstretched hand. "What is it?"

"Do you hear that?"

"Hear what?"

"That...song. Do you hear someone singing?"

Mother smiled softly then shook her head. "The king and

the land are one. That has always been true. You carry the blood of the king. It is the land speaking to you."

"The land?"

She nodded. "The realm. Britannia."

"What should I do?"

"Listen," she said then motioned for me to follow.

I pulled my hand back. I had heard such whispers before, deep within my cave, but I always thought them echoes of the past, echoes of Merlin's time there, echoes of his magic. But the land? Britannia?

Shifting my bag, I held the parcel against me, the dragon egg pressed against my chest. I followed Mother. It seemed like it took forever before we finally met the road. We turned, following the narrow cart path. Soon, farms appeared on the horizon. As we drew close, I watched men work the fields, children run after geese, and women hang linens out to dry. I stared at them. Their voices carried on the breeze and were sweet to my ears.

I've been the farmer in the field, the voice sang once more.

I stared at the scene. I had been alone for so long. Since I'd never really known the company of anyone save Mother, maybe it had made things easier. But now... What did it mean to be among people? The thought that Mother was taking me somewhere else where I would be secluded, cut off from the rest of the world, filled me with despair.

We walked away from the farm toward a small village on the horizon. We passed through a glade thick with white-barked birch trees. The leaves shivered and whispered as we strolled by. I slowed and bent my ear to the lightest sound of a song in the leaves soft voices: *Your knight. Your knight? A princess needs a knight. I've been the maiden of the lake.*

"Rapunzel," Mother called, motioning for me to catch up.

I reached out and touched the dancing leaves then raced to Mother.

"We will go to the airship platform," she said, pointing to a tall tower at the other end of the village. "We'll take a transport to London."

I gasped. "To London?"

Mother nodded. "Just keep quiet. Let me do the talking, and try to keep them calm," she said, looking down at the crate.

"Okay," I whispered, trying not to stare at everything I saw as we entered the village. But it was hard. Women hurried quickly through the square carrying baskets full of bread. Pretty ladies in fashionable hats stopped and gazed longingly at a gown displayed in the dressmaker's window. An odd machine sitting outside a blacksmith's shop whistled and popped. Its large gears turned, the smoke stack hissing out plumes of steam. A moving tray rolled, and brand new horseshoes conveyed from the machine. As we passed the carriage station, I eyed the building with curiosity. Was this where Ewan had been? More, was this where the dragon blood had been? I cast a glance around. No one here looked suspicious. In fact, everyone just looked worn thin.

Once more, the land whispered to me. *Weary. Weary. I've been the spinner at the wheel.*

I clutched my bag against my chest and hurried behind Mother.

We were just leaving the town square when I spotted a man with a cart full of books. I slowed as we passed, tilting my head to read the spines.

"Like something to read, miss? How about a romance? Or would you like something a bit darker, a gothic novel perhaps? Poetry? A Bible?"

"Do you have any books by Miss Austen?" I asked.

Upon hearing my voice, Mother stopped. She smothered an annoyed expression on her face then rejoined me.

"Oh, yes. Popular, of course. Someone just traded me," he

said, his fingers dancing across the spines. "Here it is. *Sense and Sensibility*. Interested?"

I looked at Mother—still in the guise of a man—who drew a coin from her pocket and pressed it toward the man.

"Very good," he said, handing the book to me. "All the young ladies love Jane Austen," the bookseller assured Mother then looked at me. "My, what beautiful eyes this young lady has," he said, staring at me.

"Good day, sir," Mother told the man stiffly then motioned for me to follow. Gripping the book and the bag, I smiled at the bookseller then hurried along behind her.

"No more stops. I'm sorry, Rapunzel," Mother whispered. "We must hurry."

"Yes. You're right. Sorry," I said, feeling both delighted and guilty all at once. I looked around the square. It felt so strange and so wonderful to be amongst the people. I felt their energy, their lifeblood. And from many, their weariness, which saddened me. The delight of passing children, however, lifted my spirits.

At the other end of the square stood a small airship tower. Above, two small ships were docked. I eyed them as they swayed. Mother went to the stationmaster and spoke in a low tone.

I knelt down and looked through the slats into the wicker cage where three very annoyed looking *cats* looked back at me.

"We're going to ride an airship," I said excitedly.

The prospect of the adventure did not seem to improve their mood.

"It will be all right. Mother will take us somewhere new. Just imagine where it might be," I said, then stuck my hand into the crate. All three dragons rubbed their heads on my hands. "Be good," I whispered, giving Wink a warning look.

She squinted her eyes then turned away. Even if she did

hate the illusion and the cage, at least she realized she needed to stay put.

"Very well, sir. This way. And your daughter, if you please," the stationmaster said, motioning for us to follow him up the steps to one of the airships hovering overhead.

We wound up the steps and down a platform to a small airship. The stationmaster spoke to the pilot, who eyed over the wicker crate mother carried.

"I don't transport livestock," he said with a sneer.

"Livestock? These are the young lady's cats," Mother replied sharply.

He grunted then motioned for us to come aboard. Mother and I went to the prow of the ship and took our seats. A few moments later, the crew untied the ship. The burner below the balloon fired, and the airship slowly turned from port.

Inside the wicker case, the cats meowed loudly. They could feel the sense of flight just like I could.

The ship ascended into the clear blue sky, the propeller kicking on in the back as the transport began its gentle ride toward London.

Handing my bag to Mother, I rose and went to the very front of the ship. I held out my arms, feeling the wind whipping all around me. The breeze pulled at my hair, but my long locks stayed in place. I closed my eyes and imagined I was soaring.

And then, I heard the wind. In a sweet and soft voice, it spoke a single word: *Pendragon.*

10
JOLLY OLD LONDON

MY EYES WIDENED AS THE CITY OF LONDON SLOWLY appeared on the horizon. First, I saw the small villages at the edges of the city. Their slate or thatch roofs dotted the vista below. Then more and more airships appeared in the sky, each with a unique marking on the balloon signifying its name. The ship we flew in boasted a sparrow on the balloon, the ship's name the same.

I stared as the familiar shapes, places I had seen in draw-ings or photographs, came into view: Saint Paul's Cathedral, Tinker's Tower, and London Bridge.

"Jolly old London," Mother said.

"It's magnificent!"

Mother smiled lightly, but that familiar tremor worried her mouth once more…even in the guise of a man who looked built to work the shipyards.

"What is it?" I asked.

Mother shook her head. "Nothing. I'm sorry, Rapunzel. We won't be going into the city. When we dock, I will arrange for another ship. I'll have you stay on board the *Sparrow* until our passage is secured."

"All right," I said, trying not to sound disappointed. It wasn't her fault, after all.

Turning back, I looked over the rail at the city below. Odd scents wafted up. I smelled dust, refuse, and people. The strange, sick smell was punctuated with the clean scents of freshly baked bread and the sweet tang of roasting meat.

Estrid sneezed.

Apparently, I wasn't the only one who found the city's perfume an unusual concoction.

The crew shouted to one another as the ship pulled into port. Working quickly, they docked the vessel and secured it in place.

"Sir," the pilot called to Mother.

Her eyes scanning the other airships, Mother hadn't heard.

"Sir," the man called again.

I tugged Mother's sleeve. "*Sir*, the pilot is calling."

Mother grinned. "Right," she said then turned and went to the man.

I watched as travelers debarked other vessels or stood in line to board a waiting transport. Massive ships hovered at the uppermost platform. The London hub, with three tower levels and dozens of airships, was a busy place. Gently lifting my wicker crate from the deck of the ship, I balanced it along the rail. A moment later, three sets of eyes looked out.

"Look, girls. See all the people?" I whispered.

Mother returned a moment later. "All right, Rapunzel. Stay put. The captain will keep an eye on you until I return. I know which ship I'm after. There," she said, pointing to an airship hovering on the platform overhead. The ship had the insignia of a wolf's head on a hammer. "I'll be back."

I set the basket down and leaned back into my seat. "All right. See you soon," I said lightly, trying not to let my worries show.

Mother turned to leave but then paused.

Turning back, she bent and looked me deep in the eyes. She smiled. Even though she wore the illusion of a man, she had the same dark eyes I knew well. "We'll be out of all this mess and safe soon," she told me, pushing a loose tuft of hair behind my ear.

I smiled at her.

"Love you," she said, kissing me on the forehead.

"Love you too."

She then turned and debarked the ship.

Sighing, I pulled out my new book. "Well, Miss Austen. Let's see what misadventures you have in store now," I said then flipped the book open to the first chapter of *Sense and Sensibility*.

WHEN SOMETHING GOES WRONG, it seems like it all happens very suddenly.

First, my stomach began to twist. My hands shook. And then a strange feeling, like being too close to a lightning strike, took over my body.

In the very same moment, the three small *cats* in the wicker crate began meowing and hissing loudly.

I looked up, pulled away from Miss Austen's depiction of the very miserable condition of the Dashwood sisters in the wake of their father's premature death to see a man standing on the platform not far from the *Sparrow*.

There was a meanness to his looks. Had I not been able to feel that there was something wrong, I most certainly could have discerned it from his features.

He was a large man with black hair and a heavy brow. He stared at me, his eyes gleaming. Sparks of red flickered in his eyes and between his fingers. I gasped. Blood of Mordred.

Again, the sisters hissed, and the box as my feet rattled.

The man's gaze went to the crate.

"No," I whispered. Dropping the book, I snatched my bag with one hand and the crate with the other. I cast a glance at the platform above. I couldn't see Mother anywhere.

I backed slowly toward the far side of the ship, stepping onto the bench. The man moved toward me.

"Oi, what you on about, miss? Get down from there before you fall," the pilot called then followed my gaze.

The dark-haired man jumped off the platform and onto the rail of the *Sparrow*.

"What the hell? Get off my ship," the pilot yelled at him.

To my shock, the dragon blood pulled out a pistol, aimed it at the pilot, and then shot.

The sound of the gunshot rang through the air.

The pilot held onto the spokes of his wheel for just a moment before he slipped to the deck of his ship. A moment later, there was panic as the people on the platform screamed and rushed in every direction. From below, I heard a guard's whistle and shouting.

My eye flashed toward the airship platform above me. I didn't see Mother anywhere.

"Come here," the man growled at me, motioning with the barrel of his pistol for me to get down.

Hooking my arm around one of the ropes that connected the balloon of the airship to the gondola, I climbed up onto the rail. "You won't shoot me."

"You sure about that?"

"Yes."

He smirked. "You're right. Now, come down. I've been looking for you for a long time, blood of Anna."

The wicker crate rattled once more as the dragons fought to get out.

The man's eyes went to the basket. "What's in there?"

I looked down the platform, hoping for a sign of Mother, but she was nowhere to be seen.

"Lookin' for your faerie guardian?" the man asked with a laugh. "Well, you're not going to find her. We've been watching her. Now, at last, we have you. Why don't you just come down from there, and we'll have a little talk."

"No," I whispered, my eyes glancing upward. Where was she?

The man laughed. "We'll be real gentle. I promise you that. Come on."

"You, hold there," an airship tower guard yelled at the dragon blood.

Frowning, the dragon blood turned once more and shot the man. The officer crumpled to the ground.

A wind blew in from the Thames, ruffling my long hair. On the breeze, I heard a soft whisper: *Your knight. A princess needs a knight.*

I heard a strange metal sound zip close by and then heard the splintering of wood. A moment later, a massive figure swept in alongside me and landed on the rail of the airship.

Gasping, I turned to find Ewan there. At once, he drew his pistol and leveled it on the dragon blood.

"Pellinore," the thug said then spat. "Like a damned fly. Get out of this, Ewan."

"Sorry. Rescuing damsels in distress is listed under Article 7, Item 22. It's a requirement. You, on the other hand, I have a license to kill, if necessary."

The dragon blood sneered then raised his weapon, aiming it at Ewan.

Ewan got his shot off first.

The dragon blood dodged, but the shot rang true, striking the man in the shoulder.

"Oi! Ewan? Why don't you dodge this," another voice called from the platform. I turned to see another man who looked very much like the first standing there. He was holding an odd-looking weapon, a sort of musket with a wide muzzle.

Ewan's eyes went wide.

"Rapunzel, hold on," Ewan said, grabbing me quickly around the waist. He activated a switch on his belt then we jumped. As we fell from the rail of the airship, the dragon blood's weapon blasted. There was a strange buzzing in the air and I saw a flash of blue light.

My arms wrapped around Ewan, I squeezed the strap of my bag and the handle on the crate held so tightly that it made my fingers hurt. I couldn't drop them. No matter what, I couldn't drop them. Ewan's device unspooled quickly. He activated a button, and the line slowed as we neared the ground.

"Mother," I said, scanning the platforms.

A shot from above rang out. A bright ball of blue light came hurtling in our direction. The ground near my feet exploded, grass and earth flying everywhere.

"Rapunzel, I need to get you out of here. Now," Ewan said. Taking me gently by the arm, he led me away from the airship towers and back toward the city.

"But my mother…"

Another shot rang out. A flash of blue light hit a lamppost nearby. The glass on the lamp exploded and the post buckled.

"We'll find her. She wouldn't want you to get hurt. We need to go. Now," he said then led me away.

11
THE PRINCESS
AND THE AGENT

"THIS WAY," EWAN SAID. LEADING ME BY THE HAND, EWAN raced toward his auto parked outside a tavern near the airship towers.

I stared back at the platform. I didn't see Mother anywhere.

Ewan opened the door for me. He reached down and set his hand on mine, taking the wicker crate from my hand.

I gazed up at him.

He gasped. "Rapunzel, your eyes."

My heart was slamming in my chest. All my nerves were on edge. Whenever I got upset, the same thing always happened. The colors in my eyes began to swim wildly, and I heard this strange buzzing in the back of my head. It was like a thousand voices were speaking at once. "Kaleidoscope eyes," I whispered.

Ewan stared at me. A moment later, he shook his head and looked down at the carrying case. "I'll secure them in the back. They'll be safer there. I promise."

Reluctantly, I let go of the carrier. From inside, there was a hiss.

"I promise I'm just trying to protect you, Estrid. Don't fire-ball me when you get out of there," he said then set the crate into the narrow space behind the front bench seat. He reached out for my other bag.

I clutched it against my chest and shook my head.

"All right then." He motioned for me to get in.

I slipped inside. The front seat of the vehicle, a bench for the driver and passenger, was covered in leather that was a soft camel color. Ewan jumped inside. He flipped a number of switches and suddenly the engine rumbled.

Not far behind us, there was a loud scream.

I looked back to see the dragon bloods working their way toward the vehicle.

"Ewan."

"Hold on," he said. Kicking dust and gravel behind it, the auto sped off, heading into the city. In the crate behind me, Luna *meowed* nervously.

"It's all right," I said, leaning back over the seat to comfort her. I stuck my fingers in through the open slat and felt a little head press against them.

The auto turned sharply to the right, my body sliding along with it until I was right alongside Ewan. I struggled to slide back to my side.

"Careful," Ewan said. Reaching around me, he pulled a harness around my waist and fastened it.

"Those men. They were—"

"Dragon bloods. Like you. Well, like you, but not like you."

"How did they find me? How did *you* find me?" My mind whirled like it was moving a million miles an hour. Mother was gone. The other dragon bloods were trying to abduct me. I was in an auto screaming down the streets of London. And to think, I'd spent the last nineteen years in a cave. I'd experienced more life in the last twenty-four hours than I ever had before.

"After I left you, I spotted Dormad in the village. Then I realized why. He wasn't up to his usual thieving. He was tracking you. Well, not you, but whomever that woman was you were with."

"My mother."

"Mother?"

"Well, she's not really my mother. She's my faerie guardian. A Seelie."

"Well, this just gets more interesting by the minute. But, yeah. Her. I tracked him. Apparently, he was hunting her. We all ended up here. That catches us up again, I think."

Ewan maneuvered his auto around the carriages and horses, dodging gentlemen in top hats and fine ladies carrying parasols. A whole world I had only ever read about in books came alive before my eyes. The sights, sounds, and smells of the city filled my senses. I looked overhead to see the airships floating by.

I was in London.

And was running for my life.

Ewan quickly drove down one narrow row then another, finally pulling his auto up outside an unremarkable row of townhouses. The machine heaved a sigh of steam when he turned the engine off.

Slipping out, he grabbed the crate, lifted it carefully, then came around and opened the door for me. Offering his hand, he helped me out of the vehicle. We climbed up the steps to the door of the building. Above the door, carved into the stone, were the letters R and M encapsulated by a circle. A man sat on the stoop outside reading a newspaper.

I glanced up and down the street. From what I could tell, this was a residential neighborhood. It was completely peaceful and silent.

"Thomas," Ewan said.

"Ewan? This is a surprise. And a guest?"

"Yes. I need to talk to Agent Hunter. Urgent."

"Urgent, eh? The dirty dozen giving you trouble?" The man chuckled which made Ewan frown. The stranger then shifted his foot oddly, and the door to the building clicked as though it had unlocked. As I studied the man's foot, I spotted a lever hidden just under his shoe. I also noticed the butt of his pistol sticking out from inside his jacket and the knife on his belt. This gentleman was certainly not a nondescript servant lingering over a newspaper while he waited for his master.

"Come with me," Ewan said gently. Taking me by the hand, he led me to the door.

We entered into the foyer of a quaint townhouse. A narrow staircase led upstairs. Lace curtains on either side of the door offered a soft view of the outside. It was silent inside save the soft sound of classical music on a scratchy-sounding paleophone playing somewhere in the house. The walls were papered with pale blue brocade in a floral design which was dotted with yellow birds and red butterflies. On one side of the room was a quaint parlor, the type in which the Bennet sisters might spend a sunny afternoon pining over Bingley and loving/detesting Darcy. On the other side appeared to be a gentlemen's study or library.

A maid dressed in a traditional black and white uniform appeared from somewhere in the back.

"Agent Goodwin," she said with a smile then motioned for us to follow her. "This way."

The serenity of the place seemed so at odds with the urgency of the situation; I didn't know what to think. She smiled and led us through the parlor where a woman wearing a red cape sat poring over a journal. She flicked her eyes toward Ewan.

"Agent Goodwin," she said, wrestling a smirk off her face.

Ewan pretended not to notice. "Agent Harper."

The maid guided us through the small alcove that led to

the kitchen. But to my surprise, she stopped and opened the door to a broom cupboard midway. Inside, a mop and broom leaned against the wall.

She nodded to Ewan.

Still holding my hand, he guided me forward.

"Ewan?" I whispered.

"It's all right," he said. We wiggled into the closet, a tight fit for two people and three dragons. Holding my crate in his arms, he nodded to the maid. "Have Thomas take my auto around the back?"

The maid nodded. "Of course, Agent," she said then closed the door. When she did so, I heard something inside the wall click and then a lamp flickered on.

"Whoa," I whispered.

"You like that? You'll love this." He set the crate between his feet. "Hold on," he said, taking me by the waist. He steadied me and the crate all at once.

I almost protested his overly familiar move when a moment later, the closet shuddered then began to drop. Quickly.

I gasped.

"It's all right," Ewan said. "It's lowering us below the city."

"Why?"

"I need to get you out of harm's way as fast as possible. This was the safest place I could think of."

The light on the wall flickered. I looked up at Ewan. He'd told me himself his job was to hunt people like me. To track them down and arrest—or kill—them. For all I knew, he was taking me to a cell somewhere. Me and my dragons could be in terrible danger. But if so, why was he looking at me like *that*? No. I was safe with Ewan. Everything in his eyes said so.

"Why are you helping me?" I whispered.

Ewan smiled. "Your hair."

"My hair?"

He grinned playfully. "Got a thing for girls with long hair.

Let's just say you take the prize. Can't let anything happen to a girl with hair like yours."

"Very funny. But seriously?"

"Seriously?"

"Yes."

"Because I'm afraid Estrid would be very angry with me if I didn't."

I huffed. "Ewan."

"Article 7, Item 22. All agents assigned to any division of Her Majesty's Secret Intelligence Services, under the auspices of the Rude Mechanicals, are required to rescue damsels in distress. Most particularly, princesses. I mean, you carry the blood of Pendragon, which kind of means you are the heir to our entire realm."

I raised an eyebrow at him.

"And because... Well, just because," he said with a soft smile.

The closet shook as it reached the bottom of the shaft.

The dragons in the crate meowed.

Ewan opened the door. Taking me by one hand and carrying the crate in the other, he led me into a corridor. There, stretched out before us, was a massive room filled with people busily working at their desks, red-robed agents rushing to and fro. Mechanical automatons walked with halting steps from station to station.

Ewan bowed theatrically. "Princess Pendragon, welcome to headquarters."

12
HEADQUARTERS

I stared at the assembly. Suddenly, I was overcome with a sense of anxiety. Were all these people just like Ewan? Would there be others here who would see I was…different? I gripped my bag tighter. What if they learned what I carried?

"You're safe here, Rapunzel. These people… We will help you," Ewan said then took my arm gently as we made our way down the row.

As we went, we got a few stray glances.

"Ewan," another agent greeted him. The man sat on the corner of the table absently munching an apple as he read a yellowed paper. I couldn't help but look at the small clockwork spider sitting on the man's shoulder. "What happened? Here for reinforcements? Which one of the dirty dozen got away this time?" the man asked with a chuckle.

I cast a glance up at Ewan, whose cheeks flushed red.

"Dozen?" the agent sitting across from the man replied. "Now, is that a baker's dozen or only twelve? Might need another agent in the division if you're up to thirteen now."

Both men laughed.

Ewan didn't answer then but simply moved toward the other end of the room.

"Look, Ewan caught one! By God, she looks ferocious," another agent called, causing a few others to look up. They chuckled.

Ewan clenched his jaw but didn't say anything.

I glared at the man who had spoken. Ewan had just saved my life. Why was everyone teasing him?

When we were out of earshot of the agents and headed down a narrow hall away from the larger room, I asked, "What's the dirty dozen they keep talking about?"

Ewan frowned. "There are twelve known dragon bloods in the realm. My division keeps tabs on them," he said then coughed uneasily. "Some of my colleagues think we Pellinores have an easy job."

"Oh," I said, then looked back at the other agents who were working busily. "But then, what do those other people watch over?"

"Werewolves, goblins, vampires, selkies, witches, and other creepy buggers. The realm is full of peculiarities. Don't see many faeries though—unless the druids are hiding them, which is probably the case. The people here are charged with keeping the realm and all her secrets safe."

Ewan led me down a series of hallways until we reached a closed office door. He pressed a button on the wall, and from behind the door, a bell chimed. A moment later, a second chime emitted from a bell on our side of the wall. Ewan lifted a cone-shaped receiver and set it on his ear. He leaned toward a slotted device attached to a pipe, which led to some copper tubes on the wall.

"Ewan Goodwin and guest. There was an incident at the towers."

Ewan listened.

"An airship pilot and a tower guard. Dragon blood took them out," he replied into the device.

He listened again.

"Yes, sir. I will. Sir…I have someone here you need to meet."

Ewan listened once more.

"Thank you."

Ewan hung up the receiver then turned and looked at me. "Well, I'm not fired. Yet."

"Yet?"

He chuckled then rubbed his hand on the back of his head. The expression on his face told me it was still a distinct possibility.

A moment later, the door opened, and a strikingly beautiful woman with long black hair wearing a red cape emerged. She eyed both of us. I noticed then that she had a scratch along the left side of her face, her left eye turned moon white.

"Agent Louvel," Ewan said, inclining his head to her.

She grinned. "Agent Goodwin…and guest," she said, eyeing me carefully. She raised her eyebrows then moved along.

"Ewan, come in," someone called from inside.

Tepidly, I followed behind Ewan after snagging the wicker case containing my dragons from his hand. I clutched it protectively.

The man behind the desk rose. He had blond hair, a well-trimmed beard, and a smattering of freckles across his nose and cheeks. His manner and dress were very formal. But there was a softness in his eyes that reassured me that he was probably not going to murder me and take my dragons straight away.

"Agent Hunter," Ewan said, giving the man a short bow. "This is Rapunzel. She is in need of sanctuary. The dragon bloods are hunting her. I was hoping the Society could arrange for safe passage for her somewhere out of the way."

"Hunting her? Why?" Agent Hunted quickly assessed me, from the crate in my hand to the bag I was clutching against my chest. His gaze stopped when he met my eyes. They lingered there.

"Well—" Ewan said, then nervously rubbed the back of his neck. "She is also a dragon blood."

Agent Hunter's brows arched. "But... That's not possible."

"The female heirs of Mordred do not manifest their dragon blood, that is true. I believe... I believe Rapunzel is a Pendragon from the line of Anna."

Agent Hunter looked at me then at the cases I carried once more. He fixed his eyes on mine, his gaze narrowing when he looked into my eyes. After a moment, his expression softened. "Rapunzel, right?" he asked.

"Yes," I nodded.

"Where was she?" Agent Hunter asked as he went to his bookshelf and pulled down a large ledger.

"Cornwall. I was tracking Dormad. I believe he was tracking Rapunzel's faerie guardian. I found Rapunzel in a cave along the shore. Dormad was not far behind."

"Faerie guardian?" Agent Hunter asked as he set the book down on the table. He looked from Ewan to me.

"Yes. The Pellinore archives speak of a faerie guardian, Seelie Court, who watched over Anna. Her name was Gothel," Ewan said then looked at me.

Agent Hunter turned to me as well.

"Yes, that's her," I said.

Agent Hunter nodded. "And where is Gothel now?"

"I don't know, sir. Gothel was transporting Rapunzel some-where by airship. Dormad and Owyr were on the platforms waiting. I didn't see Morad or any of the others. It's possible they picked Gothel up. Or she may have escaped to the Otherworld."

"Or they killed her," Agent Hunter said with a frown.

"No," I interjected.

Both of them looked at me.

"She's alive."

"How do you know?" Ewan asked.

I looked down at my clothes. "Her illusions are still in place."

Ewan looked back at the crate. From inside, Estrid meowed.

Agent Hunter's eyes went to the crate.

Unconsciously, I swung the crate behind me. "My cats," I said, casting a quick but pleading glance at Ewan.

To my surprise, he didn't interject.

Agent Hunter nodded then turned back to his book and began turning pages. As he did so, I glanced at the tome. Within were lineage charts. Pages upon and pages of lineage charts. Agent Hunter followed along lines which stopped. He flipped pages again, following lines that ended once more. He shook his head. "I do not pretend to be an expert on the work of your division, Agent Goodwin, but I was told that the line of Anna was extinguished."

"So we thought it was. Somewhere along the way, we missed someone. But Gothel didn't, and it has been nine generations."

"Nine generations," Agent Hunter repeated then stared off into the distance. "The Scrolls of Merlin."

Ewan nodded.

Agent Hunter looked at me. "Do you know where Gothel was taking you?"

I shook my head.

"We need to get her off the map. Some place they won't think to look for her," Ewan said.

"And then?" Agent Hunter asked.

Ewan exhaled deeply. "It is the duty of the Pellinores to watch over the line of Pendragon. But we're only three agents.

I know the rest of the agency thinks what we do is a joke. Between Lucy, William, and me, we have been keeping the dragon bloods in check. But we have never had a situation like this. I am a Pellinore—in name and in blood—and I will protect Arthur's line as is my sworn duty," he said with more earnestness than I had ever heard from him before.

"Send word to Lucy and William. Your division must be proactive in this matter. Her presence changes everything."

"Yes, sir."

"I will need to inform Her Majesty. It's not every day that someone who could literally draw the sword from the stone walks into my office," Agent Hunter said with a soft smile.

"Of course, sir."

Agent Hunter pulled a piece of paper out of his desk drawer and quickly dashed a note on it. He handed it to Ewan.

"This is the address and directions to my country estate, Willowbrook Park. Take her there. I have a small but trust-worthy staff. They will look after you." He opened yet another drawer, from which he pulled a small box. He took out a key and handed it to Ewan. "The key to the grandfather clock in the library."

Ewan raised an eyebrow then nodded. "Very well, sir. Thank you."

Agent Hunter looked pensive. "We must discover what happened to Gothel. There are very few of the golden court in the mortal realm."

"She was planning to talk to someone on another airship. I don't know who, but the airship had a hammer with a wolf's head on its balloon."

Agent Hunter stared at me, chuckled lightly, then nodded. Raising a finger, he picked up a receiver like the one in the hall and pressed some buttons. A moment later, I heard the voice of the upstairs maid. "Yes, sir?"

"Has Agent Louvel left yet?"

"No, sir."

"Please ask her to come back. I have a surprise for her."

"Of course, sir."

Agent Hunter clicked off the device and nodded to Ewan. "We'll find Gothel," he told me reassuringly then turned to Ewan. "I'll be in touch soon. For now, go to Willowbrook, and we'll go from there."

"Thank you, sir."

Ewan turned and motioned to me that it was time to go.

"Miss Pendragon, I wish you all the best. Agent Goodwin will look after you and your *cats*," Agent Hunter said.

Did he know? "Thank you."

Ewan and I turned then and headed out of Agent Hunter's office.

So, we were headed to Willowbrook Park. I liked the sound of it. I smiled, imagining Missus Bennet, Elizabeth Bennet's mother, clasping her hands in excited glee for the turnabout in circumstance. Somehow in my series of unfortunate events, I would go from cave dweller to resident of an exquisite estate. Now, if only I could find my Mister Darcy.

No. Not Darcy.

I smiled at Ewan as I followed along behind him.

Someone just like Ewan.

13
WILLOWBROOK PARK

Ewan left messages for his colleagues with the upstairs maid, and then we loaded back into his auto. He topped off the cylinders under the hood with water, and we were off once more.

There was something both terrifying and magical about riding in the auto with Ewan across a countryside. The trees, fields, and small villages felt foreign and familiar all at once. I had read about such beauty in my books, imagined it so well it had come to life in my mind. As I gazed out onto the land, I could feel its energy. It felt alive within me. And when I listened, really listened, I heard the softest of songs.

The breeze from the auto, however, did not respond well to my excessive locks. In no time, long strands were blowing wildly in the breeze.

"Here," Ewan said, pulling a scarf from his glove compartment. "Try this. You're waving your banner."

I attempted to hem in the untidy strands, stuffing them under the pretty scarf. It was a lovely thing, large enough to be a shawl, really, with pink and blue flowers. I couldn't help but catch the scent of perfume on the soft fabric. To my surprise, it evoked my jealousy.

"Your betrothed's?" I asked as I stuffed the last strand under the silk.

Ewan shook his head, and for a moment, an odd, dark expression crossed his face. "No."

"Oh," I said, sensing I'd stumbled upon something I should not have.

Ewan smiled gently at me as he looked me over. "Looks pretty on you."

I grinned stupidly which made Ewan chuckle.

Oh, Elizabeth Bennet, I am terrible at this game. My fine eyes hide nothing. Hidden away in my cave, I never had a need to mask my feelings. Everything I thought was written plainly on my face. At least I was honest. That was a positive attribute, right?

I fingered the silk tied at my chin. Okay, so if not a girl-friend's scarf, then whose?

We rode throughout the day. At some point, I must have nodded off because it was already dark when Ewan made a turn through a set of elaborate, wrought-iron gates and down the winding lane.

Trapped in the carrier all day, the girls were meowing loudly, complaining of tiredness and hunger.

"We're almost there," I reassured them. "As soon as we're safe, I'll let you out. I promise." I turned to Ewan. "Back in Agent Hunter's office, why didn't you tell him about the dragons?"

Ewan shrugged. "Fancied he wouldn't believe me, I guess. As you may have noticed, not everyone in my division is respectful of our work."

I had noticed the teasing, but Agent Hunter was the serious type. He most definitely would have believed Ewan. That meant either I had misjudged the agent, or Ewan wasn't telling the truth. If he was lying about his reason, why so?

We made the last turn around a large pond, and the three-story mansion at Willowbrook Park appeared on the horizon. It was a massive stone structure built of blond-colored bricks with arching windows. Beautifully manicured grounds surrounded the place. A pond close to the front door reflected the night's sky above like a mirror. There was the soft scent of jasmine in the summer breeze. Behind the mansion, I spotted the tops of trees in what looked like a thick forest.

"Just like Pemberley," I whispered.

Ewan turned and looked at me. "Pemberley?" he asked with a chuckle. "You know there is no such place, right? She made that up."

"What do you mean?"

"Jane Austen got the inspiration for Pemberley from an estate called Chatsworth House in Derbyshire. We're not that far from it, in fact."

"And just how do you know where Miss Austen got her inspiration?"

"I read the book. Liked it. So I just poked around a bit to learn about the author."

"Wait, you read *Pride and Prejudice*?"

Ewan shrugged. "What? It's a popular book—a bit dated now though—but I wanted to see what all the fuss was about."

Ewan pulled his auto to a stop near the front entrance.

There were only a few lights on inside. I watched through the windows as a man carrying a lamp approached the door.

"Stay here," Ewan said as he slid out of the car. He scanned the surroundings, making sure everything was as safe, then went to the house.

A butler arrived just as Ewan approached the building. The two spoke in low tones. A moment later, the butler disappeared, and Ewan returned.

"All set. The butler went to rouse the maid and cook.

They'll get rooms ready for us and a bite to eat. My colleagues will probably arrive sometime tomorrow."

I nodded tiredly then follow Ewan into the massive estate house. It was every bit like I had imagined it would be. The floors were made of polished marble and covered with luxurious Turkish rugs, the walls painted pale blue, oil paintings and portraits on the walls. Everywhere I looked, I saw wealth and comfort.

"Are you sure Willowbrook wasn't the inspiration of Pemberley?" I whispered to Ewan.

"I agree, it does seem reminiscent. The better question is why my boss works at the agency when he's this rich."

I chuckled as I gazed around. Ewan had a point. From the grand piano to the blown glass lamps, everything was exceedingly beautiful. Not a bad place for a cave dweller like me to stay for a while.

"Agent Goodwin? Please allow me to show you to your rooms," the butler called. "It's you and Miss…"

"Penn," Ewan answered for me. "Miss Penn."

"Very well," the butler said then reached out for my bag. "May I, miss?"

I clutched the bag containing the dragon egg close to me. "No, sir."

The butler look confused but only smiled and nodded. "As you wish, miss. Now, please, come along. I am very sorry we were not prepared. Master Hunter didn't inform us that you were coming. The cook is making some dinner."

"Please, nothing elaborate. It was a long ride from London, and Miss Penn needs some rest."

"Very well. We'll have it delivered to your rooms," he said then waved for us to follow him up the steps. Candlelight cast blobs of light on the glimmering marble stairs, making the crystals hanging from the wall sconces shimmer with incandescent light. We wound our way up the steps to the second floor then down a long hallway.

"Per your request, Agent, I have given you and Miss Penn adjoining bedchambers. Fresh linens have been put on the beds. The maid will be by after a bit with towels and other items for your comfort. And you said to expect two more agents?"

"Yes, within the next few days."

"Very well. We'll prepare rooms for them as well."

"Can I bring you anything, Miss Penn?" the butler asked.

"Maybe... Do you have any fish? For my cats," I said, motioning to the crate Ewan was carrying.

"Of course."

"And some tea?" I asked.

"Naturally," he said with a friendly smile then opened the door to the prettiest bedroom I had ever seen—well, imagined, more like.

The large four-poster bed had pale pink and gold curtains, the blankets and pillows matching. The walls were painted in a soft gold color. Windows opened up to a balcony that looked out on the back lawn. Though it was dark, the moon cast silver beams on the expansive gardens and fountains.

"Is that a hedge maze?" I asked, looking out on the deliciously manicured grounds.

"Indeed it is. Tomorrow, be sure to take in the grounds. They are quite lovely this time of year. And you, Agent Goodwin." He indicated a door at the back of my room. "Through here you will find your own room," he said then gave a slight cough.

"Thank you. Miss Penn is my ward," Ewan told the man, but there was a hint of discomfort in his voice.

"Of course, Agent," the man said.

My back turned to them, I hadn't seen the looks that had been exchanged, but I'd heard the unspoken words. Two unmarried people sharing an adjoining bedroom was scandalous. That was obvious even to a cave dweller like me.

I stared out at the lawn. Lightning bugs glowed as they flew through the flowers. I opened the latch on the window and let in the fresh summer air. I felt the wind on my face. It reminded me of the sea breeze that always blew into my cave.

Mother—Gothel—where are you?

The door to my bedchamber clicked shut as the butler left.

I knelt down and unhooked the latch on the wicker case. At once, Luna, Estrid, and Wink appeared, still in cat form.

Luna rushed to me at once, crawling into my arms. The others looked around, uncertain what to think. I sat down on the floor with them, petting them to comfort them.

Ewan approached, a water pitcher and basin in his hand. He poured some water into the bowl and set it down. Luna scampered out of my hand and went to get a drink.

Sitting cross-legged, Ewan joined me on the floor.

Estrid gave him a sidelong look. Even in tabby cat form, her golden eyes sparkled with menacing light. She and Wink also went to get a drink.

Ewan reached into his pocket and pulled something out which he handed to me.

It was his shard from Excalibur.

"I didn't tell Agent Hunter about the dragons because you, *Miss Penn*, are a descendant of King Arthur, a real and true descendant. I am a Pellinore—in vocation and lineage. I am descended from King Pellinore himself. Pellinore once defeated Arthur in a duel, but in the process, Pellinore damaged the holy blade Excalibur. Pellinore and Arthur made amends thereafter, but Arthur let Pellinore keep the shard as a memento of the only time Arthur had ever been defeated in battle—save when he was defeated by Mordred, his own son. King Pellinore passed the shard onto his daughter Dindraine who was—"

"The Grail Maiden."

Ewan nodded. "Dindraine passed it on to her son, and him to his, and down and down until my grandfather, my father, and then me. Everyone in my family has served this realm. As one of the Knights of the Round Table, King Pellinore swore to protect Arthur. We Pellinores existed before the Red Cape Society, even before the Rude Mechanicals. We are the original guardians, the last Knights of the Round Table. I didn't tell Agent Hunter about your dragons because I have sworn my blood, my life, to protect Arthur's legacy. It is a promise that extends beyond my badge. For the first time in nine generations, a dragon caller has been born—as Merlin prophesized in his scrolls—and I am bound by blood and honor to protect you."

"There was a prophecy? About me?"

Ewan nodded. Tepidly, he reached out and pet Luna, who gave him a sidelong glance but permitted his touch. "Yes."

"And what does it say?"

"That the blood of Pendragon will awaken, and that you will change the course of history. Others will try to stop you. But the line of Pellinore—and the Knights of the Round Table —will keep you safe. So, you see, I was destined to find you and to protect you. I won't let any harm come to you. I won't do anything to put you at risk. Do you understand?"

"I... Yes."

There was a knock on the door. "Miss Penn?" a soft, feminine voice called.

Ewan rose. "I'll go freshen up a bit," he said, motioning to his face. I had noticed that there was a ring of dirt around his eyes where he'd been wearing his driving goggles. "I'll be right next door. If you need anything, just—"

"Scream?"

Ewan laughed. "Please don't scream. I'll probably accidentally end up shooting someone."

I giggled as I rose to my feet. "All right."

With a nod, Ewan turned and left. I went to the door to greet the maid, who dropped a curtsey when she saw me. She then entered pushing a cart. "I've got tea, biscuits, and the cook is making some fish. Mister Lawrence said you came in with just one bag. No matter. Have a look," she said, walking quickly past me to a wardrobe at the side of the room. She pulled open the doors to reveal a row of dozens of pretty dresses.

"Oh," I gushed happily. Just like *all the young ladies* wore.

"Wear any one you want. Master Hunter, Sr. had a young ward who ran off to Europe to become an artist or something. She won't be back. Oh! Are these your cats? I love cats," the maid said, rushing over to the girls and scooping Estrid up before the little dragon had a chance to protest with more than a meow and flick of her tail. "Oh, little fuzzy girl. Fuzzy baby. Aren't you the sweetest?"

I tried but failed to suppress a laugh.

Estrid turned and looked at me, an annoyed expression on her face. She squirmed, quickly untangling herself from the maid.

Grinning, the maid looked back at me. "Oh, Miss Penn, your hair is so lovely. My word, it looks like spun gold. Let me draw you a bath, and we'll wash those lovely locks!"

Before I could protest, the girl briskly got underway. I sat down on the bed and petted Estrid, who was watching the maid suspiciously. I cast a glance toward Ewan's door, thinking about my knight in dusty armor on the other side.

A knight.

A real Knight of the Round Table had come to protect me.

Something told me the Bennet girls would approve.

14
ONCE UPON A TIME

LATER THAT NIGHT, AFTER THE GIRLS HAD EATEN AND HAD A chance to stretch, I dressed into a simple sleeping gown and crawled into bed. The maid, whose name turned out to be Caroline, had helped me wash out my long locks which now smelled of soap and lavender. After washing in the cave pool, dodging fish and diving dragons, it was an entirely new experience to soak in a warm basin. Despite the new, material comforts, I still couldn't fall asleep. It was almost as if the bed was too comfortable. The rich covers and nightdress were too soft. I missed my little cot built into the cave wall, the soft sounds of the water trickling down the stalactites, the smell of the earth and minerals. And I missed my books which always helped me sleep when my mind was too busy. I had left the copy of *Sense and Sensibility* behind during my hasty escape from the *Sparrow*.

My thoughts turned once more to Mother. Surely she was all right. She was, after all, a faerie. She could easily slip away, right? Mother had always managed. I eyed the cats who lay curled up all around me. The enchantments were still in place.

Gothel was alive and well somewhere. But how would she ever find me?

Sighing, I slipped out of bed and went to the window once more. I stared across the moonlight landscape. Opening the windows, I stepped outside on the balcony.

Closing my eyes, I inhaled deeply. The sweet scents of flowers and grass filled my senses.

Gothel? I whispered in my mind. *Mother? Where are you?*

I neither felt nor heard anything save the soft voice of the breeze and the sound of the leaves in the trees. Perhaps Mother couldn't hear me. But maybe the land could.

"The land and the king are one," I said. Maybe, just maybe…

"Whisper to Gothel. Tell her Willowbrook Park," I called lightly to the wind.

The air around me swirled, and I heard the sounds of insects, owls, leaves, grass, and wind. I reached out with my senses, feeling the land, the realm. Britannia. The land and the king were one. I was one with the realm. I quieted my mind and listened to the voices on the breeze, in the rustle of the trees, in the call of the night birds. I felt the realm, both outside of me and within me. I felt alive with its magic.

"Rapunzel?" Ewan called lightly, knocking on our shared door. Before I could answer, the door opened with a soft click, and Ewan stepped into the room. "I heard a noise. Are you all right?"

I turned to him. "Sorry, couldn't sleep. I'm just worried about Mother."

Ewan stood frozen, staring at me with the oddest expression on his face.

"What is it?" I whispered.

"Your eyes…they're glowing. And your hair…"

I looked down at my long locks that I had left unbraided.

They trailed behind me across the floor to the bed where they lay in a heap. I saw what he meant. My tresses had a silvery shimmer. "Just the moonlight reflecting on them," I said then looked back outside once more. My hair *was* glowing oddly. Why?

Ewan coughed uncomfortably but said nothing more. He merely joined me on the balcony. "So, couldn't sleep?"

"No. I usually read, but I left my book on the *Sparrow*. Not used to making hasty escapes. I'll have to add 'grab your book' to my list of things to remember during Article 7, Section 22 rescues."

"Item 22, not section 22."

I chuckled. "Sorry. *Item* 22."

"Another Jane Austen novel?"

"*Sense and Sensibility*."

"Ah, the Dashwood sisters."

"You know it?"

"Of course. I am a connoisseur of all the best romantic literature."

I chuckled. "You still haven't told me why, really."

"Why? Well, how is a man expected to learn what a woman really wants unless he has a look inside the female mind? Miss Austen's works are very obliging in that matter."

"Really? And what did you learn?"

"That knights in shining armor are still in fashion. I did make a very dashing entrance on the rail of that airship, wouldn't you say? I really should wear my red cape. It would have billowed magnificently."

"I *might* say that if you didn't seem so pleased with yourself about it."

"And humility, of course, is always in good form."

We both chuckled.

"Do you want me to tell you what happens in the book?" Ewan offered.

I turned to him. "I'd like that."

Collecting a handful of my hair, I sat down on the balcony floor and leaned against the rail, Ewan sitting beside me.

"Where did you leave off?" he asked.

I grinned. "Start at the beginning."

"Once upon a time—"

"It did not start with 'Once upon a time.'"

"No? It should have. All the best stories do. Now, where was I? Once upon a time…"

15
JUST ONE KISS

Ewan stayed with me, relaying the misfortunes of Marianne and Elinor Dashwood—the heroines of *Sense and Sensibility*—until my eyes finally started drifting closed. I was half asleep when Ewan finally held out his hand and led me back to bed.

"You don't even need a blanket with hair like that," he said with a laugh as he covered me.

I smiled but was too tired to respond.

I heard Ewan close the window and check the locks before returning to his room. I heard his door squeak, but not the tell-tale click of it closing. Through the slits of my eyes, I could see he'd left the door ajar.

He really did want to protect me.

The thought comforted me, but also set my mind to work. All my life, someone had been protecting me. Maybe I was special. Maybe I was the descendant of King Arthur—who was very special. But if I was, that also meant I had a fierce strength living deep inside of me. Maybe I needed to start protecting myself for a change. I was, after all, a Pendragon.

Estrid nudged under my neck, a dragon/cat scarf once more. Only a Pendragon would have a dragon lapdog I thought with a chuckle, and then I drifted off to sleep.

———

Rays of sunlight shone in through the tall windows. I woke feeling groggy and disoriented, unsure where I was for a moment. A soft little nose pressed the palm of my hand, and I sighed reassuringly, stroking the tiny dragon's ears, feeling the ridges on her back, and the familiar shifting sensation of her scales.

I was about to drift off back to sleep when my mind tripped over my senses.

Gasping, I sat up.

Estrid tumbled from my neck and landed in my lap on her back, giving me a tired but frustrated huff, which sent a puff of smoke drifting across the bed and up toward the brocade fabric overhead.

I glanced across the room to the settee where the clothes I had been wearing yesterday sat folded: a petticoat and a worn bodice.

"Mother," I whispered then glanced down at my dragons. Not cats, dragons. "Ewan!"

I heard the bed in the other room creak then a sound like Ewan might have fallen on the floor. He appeared a moment later in a pair of sleep trousers, brandishing his pistol in front of him.

"Rapunzel? What is it?" he asked, scanning the room, his weapon ready. He looked all around, his eyes finally resting on the three dragons sitting in my lap.

Wink clicked loudly, her calls quick and anxious. She wanted to go look for Mother.

"No," I told her. "We have no idea where she might be. Stay here."

There was a knock on the door. "Miss Penn?"

It was the maid.

Ewan motioned to me to stay quiet. He went to the door as I quickly grabbed all three dragons and shoved them under the blankets.

"Oh! Mister Goodwin," I heard the maid exclaim when Ewan opened the door.

I turned from the dragons to Ewan who was standing in my doorway—mostly undressed.

"Oh my God," I whispered then chuckled as I felt my cheeks redden. I had never even been kissed before, let alone…that.

A moment later, he closed the door. "She'll be back with some tea. Rapunzel, what happened?" he asked, setting his pistol on the dresser. He rushed back across the room and sat on the edge of my bed. He took my hand. "The enchantments."

"I don't know," I whispered.

Slowly, the three little bundles under the blanket reemerged. They clicked and called to one another.

Ewan rubbed the back of his neck as he thought. "Maybe Gothel went back to the Otherworld. If she left this realm, her enchantments would falter."

"Or…" I whispered.

Ewan shook his head. "Don't think the worst. Agent Hunter sent Agent Louvel to find her. Louvel never misses her mark. We'll find out where Gothel is very soon. Don't worry. I'm sure everything will be okay," he said, rubbing his fingers on the back of my hand reassuringly.

I glanced from the dragons to Ewan, taking in his athletic form, the ripple of muscles on his stomach, his firm chest, and the smattering of dark hair on it which trailed down low to... The sight of him in such a state made dragon-sized butterflies go fluttering around my stomach.

Estrid chirped, happy to have her wings back, flew to the window and looked outside. She called to her sisters, who wiggled out from under the blanket to join her.

"The grounds are expansive here. I think...I think we could take them outside."

"Now? In the daylight?"

Ewan nodded. "Willowbrook is a huge estate. Beyond the gardens are fields and a forest."

"How do you know?"

Motioning for me to follow him, and still holding my hand, Ewan led me from my bedroom through the adjoining door into his chamber. His bedchamber was distinctly masculine. The walls were made of dark wood panels, the furniture a match. Heavy green velvet draped his bed and the windows. Oil paintings depicting wildlife ornamented the walls. Except on one wall—the one to which Ewan led me—there was an illustrated map of the estate. The map was massive, taking up half the wall. Someone had lovingly drawn the entire park, trimming the images with gold filigree. It was a pretty piece that had become yellowed by time. Ewan was right. The grounds around Willowbrook were Pemberley sized.

"They never get out in the sunshine. They only went out at night. If you think it's safe... They'd love it."

"Then let's try it," Ewan said with a smile. "I'll ask the staff to make us up a picnic breakfast. We can eat outside."

I grinned at Ewan. "I think the Bennet and Dashwood ladies would approve of your plan. Did Miss Austen teach you that women like such things?"

Ewan grinned, but an unexpected look of sorrow flashed behind his eyes. He smothered it. "Of course, but—and no offense—I think I've finally won *you* over. It's Estrid I'm trying to please."

From the other room, I heard a click and snort.

"I'd swear she understands me," Ewan said, looking back toward the door.

"Why would you think she didn't?"

He looked at me.

I shrugged.

Ewan smiled then looked down at his bare chest. "I suppose I should put on some clothes if we're planning an outing."

A blush rose to my cheeks.

Ewan motioned to my locks. "Need help braiding?"

I shook my head then began bundling up my tresses.

Ewan rubbed his chin thoughtfully. "This might take a while. Should I ask for lunch instead?"

"Very funny. I'll be ready before you are."

"Want to bet?" Ewan asked.

"Absolutely," I replied.

"Okay, if I'm right—and I will be—you'll owe me..." Ewan began, tapping his chin as he thought.

A kiss? Wait, what?

"...ah, I know. You'll tell me what's in your bag," Ewan finished.

I tried not to look disappointed. "Fine." *Wait. Fine? No! I couldn't tell him about the egg, could I?*

"And I'll owe you?" Ewan asked.

"I'll think of something," I said with a grin, unable to stop my eyes from drifting down his bare chest once more.

To my shock, Ewan blushed. "O-okay," he stammered.

I looked away. *Oh my gosh. Oh, no. Elizabeth Bennet would definitely not ogle Darcy like that, would she?*

"All right then, are you ready?" Ewan asked.

I nodded.

"3...2...1."

Gathering up my hair, I turned and fled his room, banging the door shut behind me. This was one race I definitely wanted to win. My heart kept conjuring up all manner of prizes I could claim from him. But in the end, it kept drifting back to one thing: a kiss.

16
THE HEART IS A MAZE

Despite my insistence that I was going to win, Ewan was right. Braiding up my hair took forever. And not only was Ewan ready before me, but he also managed to dress and procure a picnic brunch before I even exited my room. Dressed in a yellow gown the color of marigolds, and my hair braided and coiled into a massive heap, I met him in the foyer. I had found a lovely embroidered and beaded bag in the wardrobe as well. I had shifted the dragon egg into it, cushioning it with the scarf Ewan had lent me. Finally ready, Ewan and I set out with my wicker *cat* carrier and a basket filled with delicious-smelling goods.

"So," Ewan said, eyeing my bag, "what's in your bag?"

"Just supplies."

"Ahh." Ewan rubbing his chin as he grinned. "You forget. You lost. The truth, please."

"No, I didn't forget. You said that if you won, I would have to tell you what was in *my* bag. You know, *my bag*, the one I left upstairs. This bag,"—I patted the pretty satchel I was carrying —"belongs to Master Hunter. As agreed, here is the truth. In my bag upstairs, you will find clothes, some old jewelry pieces, a jar of moonstones, some amethyst crystals, and an old Celtic coin."

"I see," Ewan said with a grin. "And in this bag?" he asked, looking at the tote I was wearing.

"Pretty, isn't it? But it's not mine, and therefore the contents are none of your business."

Ewan chuckled. "That is a technicality. You're cheating."

"I am not."

"You most certainly are too. Let's ask Diana and see what she thinks," Ewan said, pointing to a fountain that depicted the Roman goddess, situated at the center of the garden. The large fountain had benches placed all around it. Four paths led away from the center fixture in the cardinal directions. One led back to the house, the other to a rose garden, the third to the hedge maze, and the last away from the manicured grounds and into the nearby forest. "Great Virgin Huntress, tell us the truth. Is Rapunzel cheating?"

A strong wind blew through the garden, stirring up the scent of roses from the nearby garden. The sun shimmered brightly. From somewhere nearby, a songbird warbled loudly.

"Interesting," Ewan said. "Seems so."

"That's not proof. That's just a stray breeze."

"You can't tell me that you, with your little dragon family and a faerie guardian, deny the voice of the gods?" Ewan asked with a smile.

"I deny the voice of the Roman gods. This is, after all, Britannia."

Ewan laughed. "Spoken like a true Pendragon."

I chuckled then glanced around. "Should we try the maze?"

"On one condition."

"And that is?"

"If I win, you will tell me what is in that satchel," he said, pointing to my bag.

"And if I win?"

"Whatever you wish."

I smiled up at Ewan. Under the warm morning sunlight, his dark hair shimmered with flecks of gold and amber. The freckles on his nose and cheeks gave a youthful appearance to his otherwise masculine square jaw. "All right." I might have lost the first bet—and wiggled my way out of the truth—but I was not going to lose this time.

Ewan nodded, and we headed toward the entrance of the tall hedge. The finely pruned shrubbery was at least four feet above my head. At the entrance to the hedge, we found ourselves presented with two possible paths.

"I'll take the left, you the right?" Ewan offered.

"Sure," I said with a grin.

From inside the case, the dragons clicked and called.

I looked back toward the mansion. There was no way anyone could see them from here. Setting the basket down, I looked inside. "No flying high…yet. If you help me figure out the maze before Ewan—and no cheating—you can eat my scone. No leaving the maze without us. Stay low, but play," I said then unlatched the cage. Estrid and Wink crept out at once. Both of them flew in small circles, delighted to play in the sunshine. Luna, however, came out more carefully. She flew at once to my shoulder, alighting in my hair. The little dragon winced in the bright sunlight.

"That, Miss Pendragon, is an unfair advantage," Ewan said.

"No parameters were set. Next time, you have to warn me in advance that dragons are not allowed."

Ewan laughed. "Fine. On your mark," he said then looked at Estrid, who was quick to come to attention.

Estrid, Wink, and I—Luna in my braid—lined up at the entrance. Estrid blew a playful smoke ring at Ewan.

"Oh, I am so beating you," Ewan told her.

Estrid clicked in reply.

"Get set. Go!" Ewan called.

We took off into the maze. Estrid and Luna quickly zipped ahead of me. I turned left then right, looking upward for the trees that lined the garden, but I quickly got turned around. When I came to a fork in the path, I stopped and waited. A moment later, Estrid then Wink appeared, Wink clicking for us to follow her. The tiny dragon sped forward on her rainbow-colored wings. Under the bright sunshine, the colors glimmered with a twinkling light I had never really noticed before. She and Estrid sped ahead. Finally deciding her sisters were having too much fun, Luna left me and joined them.

The maze was far larger inside than it looked. Even the girls got turned around once or twice.

"Rapunzel! Rapunzel, you should have left a trail of hair," Ewan called from somewhere in the distance.

"Laugh now," I called playfully.

Giggling, I raced through the maze, all of us enjoying the feel of the sun and the breeze on our skin. In truth, we had all suffered because of our confinement. Maybe the dragon bloods would find me. Maybe I would end up being killed, but at least I'd had a chance to live just a little.

Wink, who had disappeared ahead of the others, hurried back and quickly called to us, guiding us down one narrow path after another. The girls dove and flew, almost swimming with one another in the air. I laughed, my heart filled with joy to see them so happy. A moment later, Wink called to me, encouraging me to hurry. In the distance, I could see the tree line at the back of the garden. I was close. Holding on to my satchel, I ran to the exit. I burst from the maze, expecting to cheer in triumph, only to find Ewan standing on the other side. He stood with his pocket watch in his hand, a smug look on his face.

"Thirty-four seconds. And that's how long I've been waiting," he said with a grin.

Breathless and giggling, I shook my head. "I admit defeat."

"Good. So, tell me…"

"Later," I said with a smile as I paused to catch my breath.

"Promise?"

"Yes. Tell me how you won. How did you figure it out so quickly?"

"Did I cheat? As in, did I slip between the bushes or something? No."

"That's a very indirect way of answering. So, how did you know which way to go?"

Taking me gently by the shoulders, Ewan turned me to face south once more. Then, setting his hands on my waist, he lifted me.

"See Diana's bow?"

I scanned the garden, catching a glimpse of the statue on the other side. "Yes. And?"

"Her arrow points to the exit," he said then set me down gently.

I turned and batted him on the shoulder. "You did cheat! You forfeit your prize."

"And if *you* had won, what would you be claiming?" he asked, his eyes settling on mine. There was a soft look in his glance, and I realized his hands were still resting on my waist.

Oh, Elizabeth Bennet, I am all a-swoon. "I hadn't decided," I lied. In truth, my heart had decided. All this talk of knights, prophecies, daring rescues, and protectors was too much like a fairy tale. I'd let it go to my head. I knew what I wanted, but my desire seemed very silly. I had just met Ewan. It was impossible to feel anything like that for him…yet.

Ewan grinned then pulled his hands back and offered me his arm. "The butler tipped me off, I confess. And I also understand that there is a very pretty meadow on the other side of this forest path. Shall we?"

I took his arm. "Cheater," I said playfully.

"Liar."

"Liar?"

"You still haven't told me what's in that bag."

"I will. I promised."

"When?"

"When the time is right."

"And when will that be?"

I glanced up at him. Could I trust him with the secret? Maybe. "We'll see."

At that, Ewan nodded. "As you wish, Princess."

17
PICNICKING WITH DRAGONS

THE GIRLS DARTED QUICKLY FROM THE MAZE INTO THE cover of the forest. During their nighttime roaming, they had no doubt played in the trees—I assumed. I had never enjoyed the same freedom they had. But playing during the daytime, amongst the leaves, under the sunlight, was an entirely new experience for them. Despite her apprehension, even Luna joined her sister flitting through the branches. I tried to calm my nerves, imagining hawks and eagles roaring down from the sky and scooping up my dragons.

But then I reminded myself that they were dragons, not kittens. If a hawk tried to snatch Estrid, it would be in for a very unpleasant surprise.

As the girls flew ahead, I stopped to pick some wildflowers growing on the forest floor. I inhaled each one, breathing deeply. They smelled of all the things I'd never known. Of earth and fields and forests and sunshine. I laced the pretty blossoms into my braid and slipped a few others into my satchel. Pausing, I bent to pull off my slippers.

"Rapunzel? Everyone all right?"

"Look at those pine needles," I said, motioning to the

blanket of rusty-pink dried pine needles lying on the ground. "Just...just give me a minute." Slipping off my stockings, I walked across the bed of dried needles. They felt soft under my feet. I moved gingerly so I didn't get poked, and scooped up pinecones, dismissing each find for a better specimen, breathing in the intoxicating forest air. I slipped the pinecones, pretty leaves, and more flowers into the satchel alongside the egg which, to my surprise, had an unusual golden glow to it under the sunlight. I took in everything, feeling the rays of sunshine shimmering down in slants from overhead and shining on my face. I breathed in the smell of the forest. It was so fresh and clean. I raised my hands into the air and felt the wind rush through my fingers.

"Rapunzel," Ewan said softly. "Did you ever leave that cave?"

"No." My eyes closed, I could hear the wind whipping through the branches. Overhead, the dragons called to one another. I heard the songs of the birds, the leaves, and every living thing in the forest. They all called to me, a soft chorus of voices:

I've been the spinner at the wheel
I'm the watcher in the wind

"Do you hear that?" I whispered. I looked back at Ewan who was staring at me.

He looked around. "Hear what?"

"That...song?"

He paused to listen. "No."

I hummed the notes, reciting the lines I'd heard, but shook my head. The song didn't make sense. The wind died down. In the distance, I heard Wink call.

Ewan smiled softly at me. "I think the meadow is just over the rise. Are you hungry?"

"Famished. Let's go," I said then moved toward the sunny horizon. For a scant moment, guilt washed over me. Shouldn't

I be worried about Mother, or the dragon bloods who wanted to kill me, or that someone might see my dragons and want to take them? But then I looked back at Ewan following along behind me toting the picnic basket, the wicker carrying case, and my forgotten slippers. He smiled to himself as he walked.

Somehow, when I looked at him, I didn't feel worried. I felt...safe.

I raced ahead to the tree line and came to stand at the edge of a wide field. At the very center was a tall oak tree. The meadow was filled with wildflowers. Butterflies with white, orange, and yellow wings flitted from blossom to blossom. There was a strong scent of grass and flowers as the summer sunlight shone down. The girls flew around one another happily, Wink calling to her sisters as she snatched asters and poppies from the field, tossing and catching them as she worked. Seeing Wink's game, Luna and Estrid joined the fun.

"Under the tree?" Ewan asked.

I nodded, and we headed toward the tall oak. "It's so beautiful here. Look at all these flowers."

"You prefer wildflowers, Miss Dashwood?" Ewan asked, referring to a famous scene in *Sense and Sensibility*.

I chuckled. "I love *any* flower. And that tree... It must be hundreds of years old."

"Knotty old oak. Suppose it was once a druid?"

"The druids did not turn into oaks. They worshiped oak trees," I said with a grin.

Ewan chuckled. "I know that. The druids are still roaming, loitering about Stonehenge, causing mischief with their secrecy and Celtic sorcery."

"Are they really?"

Ewan nodded. "Thank Diana, they're not on my beat. Maybe a dryad lives in this tree. Suppose we should go flush her out?"

I elbowed Ewan in the ribs.

"What? Hey, it's not outside the realm of possibility. I'm sure there are dryads—or at least, there once were. Maybe we just can't see them."

"*You* can't see them," I said with a playful wink. "Do you mean to tell me you don't see that troupe of dryads dancing around the tree trunk?"

Ewan stopped and looked from the tree to me. "Rapun—"

Laughing, pleased to see I had fooled him utterly, I snatched the picnic basket from his hand and scampered toward the tree. Ewan rushed along behind me. Setting down the basket and securing my satchel beside me, I laid down and looked up at the branches of the old oak. It really was ancient, and I could easily imagine that it was once part of druidic worship—dryads or no dryads.

I closed my eyes and listened.

Ewan sat down beside me and opened the basket. I could hear his soft breath. I could hear the leaves shifting overhead. I could hear the insects. I could feel the tree, its broad limbs, its deep roots. Again, I heard a soft song, as if someone was singing but too far away to catch the full song.

I sat up and looked around.

"What is it?" Ewan asked.

I scanned the horizon. Birds flitted through the trees, butterflies danced, and three dragons collected flowers, but otherwise, we were alone.

I shook my head. "Nothing. Probably just dryads playing games. So, what do we have?" I popped up on my knees to investigate the picnic basket.

Ewan snapped out an embroidered cloth and began unpacking the treats from the basket onto the picnic blanket. First, he set out a basket in which was a variety of baked goods, and then he removed a parcel containing apricots, cherries, and blueberries. I snatched an apricot, delighting in its sweet taste as I watched the girls play.

"Oh yes," Ewan said as he lifted a pot from the basket. "Now, here we go."

"What is it?" I asked.

Ewan opened the pot. Inside were bangers and thick slices of bacon. The smoky scent of the meat effervesced from the container. "Seriously, Rapunzel. Why my boss lives in London rather than at Willowbrook is a mystery to me...well, save Agent Louvel. Just look at this," Ewan said as he went digging for a knife.

"Agent Louvel?"

He nodded as he worked. He sliced open a round of sourdough bread—which I was pretty sure was intended for two people. Inside, he layered the sausage, bacon, a hardboiled egg which he cut in half, more bacon, and then some cheese. "His girlfriend. The werewolf hunter."

"Love is a good enough reason," I said, grinning as I watched Ewan struggle to hold his creation. "I think you could get a few more slices of bacon on there," I said, fighting to hold back my laugh.

"You think so?" he replied in all seriousness, looking from the mostly-empty pot to his bread creation.

I couldn't hold back. A laugh escaped me. "No, I do not. Ewan! You'll never be able to eat all that."

He raised his eyebrows then nodded. "Watch me. There is nothing better in this world than bacon. The fact that it is my boss's bacon, which I am eating for free, makes it all the more delicious. Try some."

"Is there any left?"

"A few slices."

"I've never eaten it before."

"What?"

"Gothel doesn't like the smell."

"But it's bacon," Ewan said, looking as shocked as if I'd just told him I didn't like pie.

I shrugged.

"You have to try it," he said. He moved to grab a piece for me but nearly lost a hunk of cheese from his sandwich.

"I got it." I lifted a piece of the crispy meat from the pot. I took a bite, letting the salty, smoky flavor fill my mouth. I'd read about bacon, of course, but never ate any because of Mother. Now, I saw why everyone loved it. "That is amazing."

"Bacon is…" Ewan began, pausing to look philosophical. "Perfection," he said then took a bite of his massive bread, meat, and cheese creation. His cheeks puffed out like a squirrel. He looked like he was having trouble chewing, but sighed contentedly all the same.

Chuckling, I shook my head then lifted an apricot and a cube of cheese from another container.

"You're missing out," Ewan said then took another massive bite.

I eyed the pot once more. "I didn't want to deprive you of a second helping."

Ewan chuckled, his mouth still full.

I snagged another piece of bacon and let the savory taste linger on my tongue.

I looked out across the field. I was amazed to see that the girls had not come rushing over the instant they heard the food containers opening. Instead, they were working busily on something. Estrid was carrying branches from the nearby forest, the others snatching flowers from the field.

"No one can resist bacon," Ewan said between chews then lifted a crispy strip of the meat. "You see. It's perfect. You can hold it daintily between two fingers like so," he said, demonstrating. "In a formal setting you use a utensil, of course. It's salty, smoky, meaty, and crunchy. And I must say, Agent Hunter's bacon is not a cheap cut. It's Pemberley bacon." He winked then sighed happily once more.

Turning back to the breakfast, I snatched another slice, sighing happily as the delicious taste filled my mouth.

"You see," he said, his mouth still full. "Can't deny the allure of bacon. Speaking of, your horde seems decidedly disinterested."

"I noticed," I said, taking another bite. "I have to agree, it's unlike them to miss a meal."

The girls flew busily to and fro, calling to one another as they dove amongst the grass on a rise not far away. Now I was curious. Stuffing the last of the bacon into my mouth, I rose, grabbed my satchel, and headed across the field to see what had the girls so distracted.

Still chewing, but his curiosity also piqued, Ewan followed me—his bread and meat creation in his hand.

We crossed the field to where the girls were working.

I stopped when I saw.

There, in a sunny spot in the field, the dragons had been busy building a nest. It wasn't complete yet, but the outline of it was clear enough. Using the tender branches Estrid had been carrying, they were building the structure of the nest, weaving flowers and soft grasses in between.

"What are they doing? Making a bed?" Ewan asked.

Estrid flicked her tail at him then eyed the last bite of Ewan's breakfast.

Ewan looked from the final bite of his bread, bacon, sausage, and cheese creation to the dragon. With a grin, he tossed it to her.

True to her mark, Estrid snatched the bite out of the air, chirping once more to him in thanks, then flew back off to the forest for more branches.

Wink headed back into the field for more flowers.

Luna, however, landed on the satchel. She nosed the fabric then looked up at me.

My heart beat hard in my chest. Ewan was there to protect

me. Maybe he needed to see everything he was guarding. After all, if something happened to me, he was the only person who could help. If something happened to me, he would have to look after the egg, especially if Gothel didn't return.

"You asked what was in my satchel." I knelt and motioned for Ewan to join me.

Luna flew up, landing on my braid, and rubbed her head under my chin.

I scratched her tummy then she flew off to join her sisters.

Opening the satchel, I lifted the egg I'd hidden inside. I had wrapped it in the scarf Ewan had lent me. I slowly removed the silk covering. Gently, I held the egg in my hands and then laid it down on the nest the sisters had built. Under the summer sun, it shone so brightly. Before it had the appearance of a milk-white crystal. Now I saw veins of gold, and the whole egg seemed to shimmer with yellow light.

"Is that… Is that a dragon egg?" Ewan whispered.

"Yes. The last one. I haven't been able to figure out how to get it to hatch." I leaned over and set my ear to the egg. I could hear the soft heartbeat inside. "The dragon is still alive, though."

"Where did you get it?"

"In Merlin's cave. The eggs were hidden there, all four of them. I hatched Estrid when I was still a girl, singing her silly songs until one day she woke. Wink woke when I sang Arthurian ballads to her. Luna…I hatched her under the moonlight. This dragon, however—" I stroked the egg. "I haven't been able to solve its mystery."

Estrid returned a moment later, a branch in her jaw. She carefully placed it in the nest then called to her sisters. Wink returned with a daisy, Luna with a sprig of wild parsley. They worked, adding their finds, then they all lay around the egg.

"It's glowing," Ewan said.

I nodded. "It's never done that before. Maybe the sunlight is warming it."

I gasped when the egg trembled.

"Did you see that?" Ewan asked.

I nodded.

"Sing to it," Ewan suggested.

"Sing what though? I've tried everything."

Ewan shrugged. "Make something up."

I set my hand on the egg. To my surprise, it was warm. "Okay, I do know one new song. I don't remember it all though. It was mentioned in *Pride and Prejudice*."

"Try it. What does it hurt to try?"

"Well," I began. "Okay." And then I began singing.

You who have tasted love's mystic spell
What is this sorrow naught can dispel?
What is this sorrow naught can dispel?
While thus I languish, wild beats my heart,
Yet from my anguish I would not part,
I seek a treasure fate still denies,
Naught else will pleasure,
Naught else I prize...

Ewan and I both stared at the egg. It still shimmered the same golden color, shining brightly in the sunlight. But not more than that.

I shook my head. "Mister Darcy would definitely frown at that rendition. I don't know its song," I said, stroking it gently.

Ewan turned and looked at me. He gasped. "Rapunzel?"

I looked up. Much to my surprise, it seemed that all the butterflies in the field had come to me. They fluttered all around me. And my hair, which did look copper-colored in the bright sunlight, had taken on an almost pink hue. But it wasn't just my hair that was glowing: a warm, rosy glow radiated off my skin.

Smiling, I stood and extended my arms. The butterflies danced playfully around me then after a few moments, flew off.

"What...was that?" Ewan asked.

I shrugged. "I don't know. Sometimes when I sing, animals are attracted to the song. And then there is this—I don't know what to call it—magic, I guess, that comes over me."

Ewan shook his head. "Beautiful."

I smirked. "Are you saying I'm beautiful?"

"Well, yeah."

That was not the answer I expected. I had expected him to say something funny or witty. A true compliment? No, I wasn't anticipating that. "Thank you. Pretty or not, still no luck," I said, gazing down at the egg.

"Well, Miss Pendragon, we'll come up with something," Ewan said. Then, he chuckled.

"What is it?"

"It just occurred to me. I am the first Pellinore to actually capture the Questing Beast...well, beasts, in their case," he said motioning from the egg to the girls. "And I don't think I've ever wanted to protect anything more in my life. Well, almost anything." He reached out and touched my chin. "Some dragon hunter I am."

I swallowed hard, trying not to let my feelings show. To hide them, I grinned. "Ewan, I have something to tell you," I whispered.

The lines around his mouth trembled. "Yes?"

"You won't laugh."

"Rapunzel... No, of course not."

"Ewan... I love bacon."

At that, Ewan laughed then placed his arm around my shoulder and pulled me close, planting a kiss on the top of my head. "Yeah. Me too."

18
WE LOVE LUCY?

WE SPENT THE MORNING LINGERING IN THE FIELD, WATCHING the egg, waiting for it to do *something*. Aside from glowing, there wasn't much to see. Once or twice the tiny creature within shifted. Part of me worried that the sun was bothering it. What if the dragon was lunar like Luna? For the love of all things holy, I could be cooking it alive. I'd thought about moving it, but the longer the egg sat in the sun, the more it glowed. That, and I trusted the girls. If they thought the egg should be in a nest in the sunniest part of the field, I wasn't going to second-guess them. In truth, the dragon seemed to be waking. Now I just needed to learn the right song. In the late afternoon, the girls—and Ewan—decided it was time for a rest. Ewan laid down under the shade of the oak tree, the girls finding cozy spots amongst the branches. I had just decided it was time to join them when a figure appeared on the other side of the meadow.

It was Estrid who first spotted the stranger. She clicked to me and let out a low growl.

"Ewan," I said, shaking his shoulder. "Wake up."

"What? What's wrong," he asked. Pulling his pistol, he rose.

"There," I said, pointing. On the other side of the field was a figure in a red cloak.

"Ewan," a husky voice called.

Ewan smiled and reholstered his gun. "It's Lucy," Ewan told me. "Lucy," he called then waved to her.

Panic gripped me. Telling Ewan about the egg, letting him see the girls, that was one thing. A stranger was something else.

I rose and turned to the girls. I was about to call to them when Ewan set his hand on my arm.

"You can trust Lucy," he said, an earnest expression on his face. "We have all sworn an oath. We Pellinores will protect you. You can trust us, trust Lucy. You'll see."

I inhaled deeply and watched the woman crossing the meadow.

"Not the egg," I whispered. "Don't tell her about the egg."

Ewan gave me a sidelong glance. "All right." Nodding to me, he rose and crossed the field to meet his partner while I went back to the little nest the girls had built to gather up the egg.

Kneeling down, I touched the egg. It was hot. "Well now, little solar dragon, are you planning to wake up soon?" I whispered.

I laid out a handkerchief and placed some of the leaves, herbs, and flowers the girls had collected onto it. Gingerly picking up the hot egg, I set in on the fabric then placed it in my satchel once more.

"We'll come again, little one. Tomorrow. I promise you. For now, I must keep you safe."

To my surprise, the egg trembled.

"Are you a silly one like your sisters? I can't wait to meet you."

But even if the dragon hatched, then what? Gothel was missing. I was already being hunted. What if the dragon bloods found me here? A newborn dragon needed protection and care. What would happen to this little one—to all of them—if they fell into the wrong hands? Estrid had grown twice her size since she was first hatched. How big would she become? In a world where the sky was filled with airships, what would happen to a grown dragon? My dragons needed me. I couldn't let anyone take them.

I sighed. Mother would know what to do. If she did not, maybe her people would. If worse came to worst, Mother could take the dragons to the land of the Seelie and keep them there. I glanced toward the forest beyond the old oak.

"Mother, where are you?" I whispered.

Again, the wind picked up. I felt the gentle breeze on my cheek and the soft sound of voices murmuring amongst the blades of grass. I returned to the oak tree once more. I glanced up at the girls. "Mind your manners. She's a friend."

Estrid huffed uncertainly while Wink opened a single eye, watching the stranger approach. Luna crept back into the shadows.

"Rapunzel," Ewan called as he and the stranger neared.

Lucy was very unlike what I expected. She was as tall as Ewan and just as broad. Her dark hair was cut short at the nape of her neck but hung long on her chest at the front, her bangs cut blunt. She wore leather trousers, a bodice, and a dark top. A red cape billowed from her shoulders. I caught the glint off the pistol hanging from her belt. She crossed the field toward me, her strides long and powerful, then bowed low.

"Blood of Anna," she said, her voice full of reverence.

"I...um...hi," I stammered.

She stood and looked me over carefully. "Dainty thing, save all that hair," she said then turned to Ewan. "Are you sure?"

"Her eyes," Ewan said.

Lucy gave me a hard look, tipping her head as if she was watching something that perplexed her. "The colors...move."

Ewan laughed. "You get used to it. And that's not all." Ewan's eyes met mine.

I glanced at Lucy once more.

Trust.

I needed to trust her, trust Ewan.

I turned from Lucy to the old oak tree. "Girls, come meet Lucy," I called.

Lucy's gaze followed mine.

From where we were standing, we couldn't make them out clearly. The tree branches rattled, and Estrid emerged from the top of the tree then glided down toward the tall woman. The air shivered, and Wink appeared, floating in the air before Lucy. Luna landed on my back. She crawled up my braid and peered at the stranger over my shoulder.

"Angels and ministers of grace," Lucy whispered, her eyes going from dragon to dragon then back to me once more. "None other than the blood of Pendragon could wake such creatures. They're...amazing." She reached out to touch Wink who, much to my surprise, permitted it.

"Watch that one though," Ewan said, pointing to Estrid. "She's feisty."

Estrid blew a smoke ring at him. I grinned, surprised to see the love-hate relationship that had blossomed between them. But then my eyes rested on Ewan once more. No, it didn't surprise me, not really. There wasn't much about Ewan that was hard to love.

"Ewan, what in the hell do we do now?" Lucy asked.

"Protect them," he said simply.

Lucy huffed a laugh. "Easier said than done. If Dormad learns she has these, there will be no stopping him. What did Agent Hunter say?"

"Well, I didn't exactly tell him about the dragons."

Lucy watched the girls who, having made their welcome, went back to rest amongst the branches of the oak once more. Lucy nodded slowly. "Good. When William comes, we Pellinores will decide. This is our mission. They have laughed at us for years. But now…"

"Exactly. Hunter did say he would have to inform Her Majesty. After all, Rapunzel is the rightful heir of the realm."

Lucy chortled. "Something tells me Victoria won't be pleased."

"Ewan…the queen… She won't be angry, will she? I mean, I don't want anything. I just want to find my mother and…I don't know…keep out of the way."

Ewan smiled reassuringly at me. "I'm sure Her Majesty will understand once she meets you."

"Her mother? But the line of Anna… I thought it was extinguished."

"She means Gothel, the faerie guardian. We think the dragon bloods picked Gothel up. Agent Hunter sent Agent Louvel after her."

Lucy laughed once more. "Dormad and Owyr have no idea who they're messing with. I hope Louvel remembers she's supposed to avoid killing them if she can," she said then bobbed her chin toward me. "Do we know who Rapunzel's real mother is? Sorry, Rapunzel, I don't mean to be rude. It's just… It is our job to mind the blood of Pendragon. Apparently, we lost someone along the way."

"It's all right," I said. "I don't remember anyone other than Gothel."

Lucy frowned. "There was that woman in Lancashire, but she never had any children."

Ewan nodded. "I thought of her too. We did lose track of that line near the Fens. Could be there. When we find Gothel, maybe she will tell us."

"Tell you…about my real mother?" I asked.

Ewan and Lucy both looked at me.

"Yes. Maybe. Let's leave off of this topic for now," Ewan said, apparently picking up on my distress. "Shall we go back? Maybe we can grab a spot of tea."

"Tea? Dragons are alive and here is a descendant of Anna in the flesh before us. Ale seems more fitting," Lucy said with a laugh.

Ewan pulled out his pocket watch. "Past midday. No reason not to. I could eat something too."

"Eat? Again?" I asked.

Lucy laughed. "I see she's got you figured out already. Miss Pendragon, if a woman ever wanted to win Ewan's heart, all she would need is—"

"Bacon," Ewan finished then winked at me.

We both laughed.

"Ale and bacon it is then. And let's be sure to eat and drink as much as we can. Boss's account, after all." Lucy looked toward the tree once more. "They coming?"

I grabbed the wicker crate and looked up at the girls. They looked so comfortable, so free. No. Enough hiding. Enough living in cages. "We're going back now," I called. "Come to the balcony of my room. Stay out of sight of the servants."

Estrid clicked, Wink chiming in after her.

"They understand you?" Lucy asked.

I nodded. "Luna?"

After a moment, I head a soft click of assent. *My brave girl.*

Ewan picked up the picnic basket then offered his arm to me. "Princess."

Lucy chuckled then gave Ewan an assessing look. I saw her eyebrows arch, but she said nothing. Together, we headed back to my personal Pemberley.

19
GETTING STOUT

I'd never been far from my dragons before. But I had also never been out of my cave, with strangers, in a manor house, served by anyone, or being watched over by a decidedly handsome man who fashioned himself a Knight of the Round Table.

Ewan spoke to the butler, and then Ewan, Lucy, and I were led to a library where Lucy and Ewan could work. A table was cleared so lunch could be served. Lucy and Ewan spoke in hushed tones, Lucy pulling scrolls, journals, and papers from a bag. Beginning to feel a bit like an item of study rather than a person, I meandered around the library looking for something with which to preoccupy myself.

On the wall was a tall oil painting of a man in a white wig and some very expensive looking pantaloons. There was just the hint of a resemblance to Agent Hunter, Ewan's boss. At the large window at the back of the room was a telescope. I set my eye to it, but in the bright light of day, there was little to see. I trained it across the garden and toward the skyline above the trees. No sign of my girls. At the bookshelves, I let my fingers dance on the rows of leather-bound books. Histories, reference texts, and books written in Latin, the books struck me as objects that had been acquired more for the show of wealth than the pleasure of reading. Each spine was unbent, each book looked like it had been shelved and never thought of again, objects of art rather than pearls of wisdom and delight. My fingers danced over the volumes until I found one that seemed interesting, a single volume of *Holinshed's Chronicles of England, Scotland, and Ireland*. I pulled the volume from the shelf and sat down in a large, comfortable chair near the window.

Apparently, Miss Austen's works were far more riveting than Holinshed's discussion of an eleventh-century Scottish nobleman, Banquo of Lochaber, a predecessor to the House of Stuart. I woke with a jolt when the butler came in pushing a cart laden with food. I grabbed the yellowing text before it tumbled to the floor. Rising, I slipped the volume back on the shelf then I went to the table where the man was setting out high tea. I smiled nicely as the butler pulled out a chair for me then poured me a cup.

Much to my surprise, neither Ewan nor Lucy had yet bothered to join me. Given Ewan's passion for food, I was surprised.

"Carrot cake?" the butler offered.

I nodded, grinning at the confection as the man slid a slice onto my plate.

"You're missing out," I called to Ewan as I unfolded my napkin.

He turned and looked at me. I was surprised to see he was wearing a pair of small, round spectacles. Quickly pulling them off and setting them aside, he looked from me to the cake then nodded affirmatively. He said something to Lucy that I didn't quite hear. She looked at me over her shoulder then gave Ewan an amused look. She nodded.

"Agent Eckle," the butler said. He crossed the room and handed Lucy a heady brown stout with a crown of foam.

"Thanks," she said, taking the cup. She stood drinking it with one hand while she sifted through the papers laid out in front of her with the other.

"Agent Goodwin? Tea, or something with a bit more backbone?"

Ewan rubbed the back of his neck. "Stout for me too."

The butler nodded.

Suddenly, I felt a bit dainty with my tea and cake while Lucy was slugging back a stout. Regardless, I took a bite. The delicious mellow flavor of the carrot cake perfectly spiced with cinnamon and molasses melted on my tongue. I held back an embarrassing moan of delight. What could I do? I was just a cave dweller with only the model of the fictional Elizabeth Bennet to guide me. Something told me that Lucy was far more modern than the Bennet sisters. Dainty or not, that cake was divine.

Ewan joined me at the table, his eyes surveying the culinary landscape with interest. He popped an iced shortbread cookie in his mouth then took a deep drink of his beer. He sat back in his seat and stared at the table, lost in his thoughts.

"And what have you uncovered?" I asked, pointing to the papers he and Lucy were considering.

"Problems, Miss Pendragon," Lucy answered.

"And possible solutions," Ewan offered.

Lucy frowned at him. "Not good ones."

"No. I didn't say they were good ones."

Both agents frowned.

"What is it?" I asked.

Ewan sighed. "Keeping you and your tiny horde safe is going to be a problem."

"Unless," Lucy said, tapping her fingers on the table.

"Unless what?"

"Unless Her Majesty grants us permission to wipe out the

blood of Mordred. Now that you're here, it changes things. But problems remain," Lucy said.

"What problems?" I asked.

"Well, the blood of Pendragon is sacred. Legend tells us that even the line of Mordred can produce a dragon caller. Unlikely, but possible. As it is, you are just one person. If you die with no heir and we've extinguished the line of Mordred, then the blood of Pendragon ends. That can't happen. Maybe if you had a child, or a gaggle of them, things would be different," Lucy said.

"If I had...a child?" I said, trying not to choke on my tea. I flashed a quick look at Ewan, who was looking at me. My cheeks reddened.

And so did his.

Lucy sniggered then said, "If we could ensure the blood of Pendragon from Arthur and Gwenhwyfar could carry on, then it might be different. But for now, it's just you. It's not your fault or anything. Timing. We'll find another way."

"Another way for what?" a voice called as a stranger entered the room. "By Christ, look at this place. Who knew Hunter was so bloody rich? Whoa, who is this lovely creature?"

I turned to see a man around the age of sixty enter the room. He was tall, lean, and wore a red cape similar to the one Lucy wore. On his chest, he wore the badge of the Pellinores.

I rose slowly.

"Rapunzel, this is William, our colleague," Ewan explained.

"Rapunzel. That's a mouthful," William said then gave me a little bow. "Now, what's all the fuss about? The messenger said it was urgent. I was tracking Gravaine, who was hot on the trail of something. He came down from Scotland so fast it was like he was on fire. Something sure had him riled up."

Lucy smirked. "Yeah. Her," she said, pointing to me.

"Her?" William replied. "What, is she his girlfriend or

something? What's she doing here? What? Why are you two grinning like that?"

Ewan chuckled then crossed the room to his colleague. Setting his hand on the man's arm, he slowly led him to me.

"William," he said gently, moving the man in front of me. "Meet our Questing Beast. Rapunzel, this is William Williamson. William, this is Rapunzel. Rapunzel Pendragon, blood of Anna."

William stared at me. "Make a stuffed bird laugh. Someone pour me a drink."

Chuckling, Ewan poured William a beer and handed it to him. "Stout?"

"Hope we bloody well are, because things are about to get interesting," William said then took a long drink, winking playfully at me over his tankard.

Ewan grinned. "If you think that's interesting, wait until you see her dragons."

William stopped mid-drink. His eyes widened. With a line of foam hanging on his moustache, he looked from Ewan to me. "Dragons?"

20
BUTTER UPON BACON

THE EVENING PASSED QUIETLY AS EWAN, LUCY, AND WILLIAM considered their next moves and to where I should be moved. As it turned out, a lot depended on Mother. But if Mother was nowhere to be found, then what?

Just after sunset, I returned to check on whether my little horde had returned, and I wanted to see to the egg in private. Luna, Estrid, and Wink were waiting on the balcony. They looked exhausted, dirty, and happy. Aside from the dirt, I felt the same. It was strange to be out in the world. As exciting and interesting as it was, it was still a lot to take in. And yet, I felt so comfortable here. Agent Hunter's library certainly needed better books, but aside from that, the halls of the mansion felt strangely like home. Maybe it was because the place was so cavernous. It was elaborate but homey all at once. I couldn't imagine why Agent Hunter didn't want to live here. It was the kind of place a person dreamed of.

I let the girls in and gave them something to eat and drink. They quickly mowed down their dinner then crawled onto the bed to sleep.

"Seems like the three of you have adjusted to Willowbrook

Park very well too," I said, laughing as Wink set her head on my pillow. "If you become as big as a carriage, and you very well might, there won't be any more sleeping in beds."

Wink clicked tiredly then closed her eyes.

Giggling, I went out on the balcony. Once again, the fireflies danced across the gardens. It was an enchanting sight to behold.

I heard the door click open behind me and listened to Ewan's footfalls as he crossed the room. Wordlessly, he came to the balcony.

"Beautiful night," I whispered, looking up at the moon.

"Yes," he said softly.

For a moment, I closed my eyes and imagined Ewan wrapping his arms around me. I was just being romantic, of course. Stuff like that only happened in fairy tales. Then I felt his hand touch the small of my back. Tingles of pleasure washed over me, and I craved to touch him more. I leaned into his shoulder. He responded by wrapping his arm gently around my waist and pulling me close to him.

He was so very tall. I felt small but safe with his arm around me.

"Well, have you decided where I should be carted off to?" I asked.

"We have a few ideas."

"This place is so lovely. I'll hate to leave."

"Can't argue with you there."

"And if I do have to go somewhere. Will you... I mean, will I have to be alone there?"

Ewan chuckled softly. "No, Rapunzel. I am your knight. I will always be by your side."

"But Ewan," I said, "surely you have your own life. You can't just drop everything because you bumped into some weird girl in a cave who just happened to have a bunch of dragons."

"I most certainly can. Especially when I was born to look after her."

"Right. Because you're a Pellinore."

Ewan shook his head then reached down and touched my cheek. "No."

"No?"

"Not because I'm a Pellinore. Because I'm me, and you're you," he said, stroking his thumb across my cheek. "Because I was waiting—not for a dragon—but for a girl who loved bacon as much as me. How could I ever let you go now? You're butter upon bacon."

"Butter upon bacon. Doesn't that mean I'm too much?"

"Yes, you are," he said then grinned at me. "You're too much to say no to. You're all the best things at once. You're better than butter upon bacon."

"Better than butter upon bacon? That's a new one," I said.

Ewan chuckled. I felt his chest shake with the movement. Again, I relished the feel of his body against mine. But his words stirred my heart. "That's a good line. Did you learn that from reading Jane Austen?"

"No, that's all Ewan Goodwin."

"Seems you're a secret romantic. You'll have to share your love of romance novels with me."

Ewan snickered softly but didn't say anything.

I turned and looked up at him. Once more, he had that odd, pained expression on his face.

"Ewan?"

He smiled softly down at me then stroked my cheek gently. "I had a younger sister," he said then. "She was only fifteen. She was the one who loved the novels. She was very ill, too ill to even hold a book. I read them to her. All of them. She... died a few years ago. I know those books because of my sister."

I stared at him. Suddenly, the pieces of the puzzle fit together. "The scarf in your auto."

"That was hers as well. Before she got sick, she used to ride with me. She wanted to join the Society when she was older," he said then shook his head. "She was a very sweet thing."

"I'm so sorry," I said, heartbroken when I saw the tears well up in his eyes.

"I miss her," he whispered.

I smiled softly at him, feeling my own nagging longing and worry for Mother rising up in me. I buried it, staying in that moment for him. I touched his cheek. "What was her name?"

He smiled. "We're Pellinores to the bone. Dindraine."

"Of course. Beautiful."

"She would have loved them," he said, motioning back to the dragons. "All the world will. But there are some who may want to use them. We must be so careful."

I nodded.

Ewan breathed in deeply then stared out at the garden. He exhaled slowly, releasing his sadness. "I've been dying to check something out ever since we got here. Up for an adventure?"

I nodded, then Ewan and I turned and headed toward the door.

Estrid, who had been sleeping under the blankets, poked her head out.

"We'll be back soon. No exploring. Got it?"

Estrid snorted then slid back under the covers.

"They're getting spoiled here."

"Them and me both," I agreed.

"Me too. And Lucy and William as well. I think they like Hunter's stout. They found the billiards room. They were there drinking when I left."

"And where are we going?"

"Oh," Ewan said teasingly as he pulled a key from inside his pocket. "Only time will tell."

21
VORTIGERN'S CASTLE

EWAN AND I HEADED BACK TO THE LIBRARY. MOTIONING FOR me to follow, he led me to the massive grandfather clock that sat along the wall.

"Remember what Agent Hunter said?" he asked.

I nodded, recalling Ewan's boss handing the key to him.

Ewan opened the glass face of the grandfather clock. On the moon dial at the top of the clock was the image of a moon with a face, its mouth open in a wide yawn. Ewan stuck the key inside. I wasn't sure what to expect, but when Ewan turned the key, a latch unlocked. To my surprise, the back panel of the grandfather clock, which was flat against the wall, swung open to reveal a narrow passage on the other side.

"False wall," Ewan said. "The agency has loads of hidden places like this all over the country. Feeling brave?"

"I'm a Pendragon, remember?" I asked with a wink.

Ewan grinned. He snatched his goggles off his belt and pulled them on. When he activated a lever on the side, a green glow surrounded his eyes. Ducking, he stepped inside and through the clock.

"Mind your hair on the pendulum and cables," Ewan said.

Gently pushing the pendulum aside, I followed Ewan within then closed the clock behind me.

The space that Ewan and I entered appeared to be a narrow space between two walls. Our path lit by Ewan's goggles, we headed down the narrow passage to a door. Ewan opened it to reveal a flight of stairs that led below the manor.

He looked back at me.

I giggled at the sight of his face illuminated green, remembering that this was how I'd first seen him. I nodded for him to go ahead.

We headed down the stone stairwell. The stairs were crudely made. The stone appeared to be carved out of the foundation of the house, the earth itself, not set by a mason. We wove further and further down. Soon, I was met by the familiar smells of minerals and earth. As we traveled, the walls had shifted from wood to stone to earth and rock. We were deep underneath the manor house now.

The light from Ewan's goggles revealed the bottom of the stairwell ahead. As we neared the end of the stairs, Ewan stopped to lift a torch from a wall sconce. Digging in his pockets, he pulled out a small device. When he clicked it, I caught the distinct scents of sulfur and flint, and the device ignited a small flame. He lit the torch then closed his machine once more, blowing on it to cool it down before he slipped it back into his pocket.

"Forgot to cool it off once," he whispered. "Caught my shirt on fire."

I giggled.

Taking my hand, he led me forward.

I knew my mind should have been fixed on whatever surprise awaited me, but all I could do was stare at Ewan, to relish the feeling of my hand in Ewan's, my skin upon his. While my life in my cave had been safe, it had been so very lonely. If not for the girls, I would have sunk into a terrible melancholy. But now... Well, now I knew what it felt like to live.

"Wow," Ewan said, lifting the torch.

Pulling myself away from my thoughts, I looked around me.

I gasped.

We were standing in the center of what appeared to be the remains of a Roman temple. Ewan lit the other torches on the walls. The room was bathed in orange light.

The temple was long, a narrow stone path down the center. On either side was a shallow pool, rectangular in shape, and only a few inches deep. Water ran down the walls of the underground temple, into the pools, and out the other end, leaving the water perpetually fresh. The walls had been carved with reliefs of a muscular man slaying a bull. All around, I saw unusual imagery intermixed with images of the same hero: discs, suns, hammers, animals. The designs were not Celtic. They barely even looked Roman. There was a strange feeling in the air. At the other end of the temple was a tall statue with the head of a lion, the body of a man, and wrapped around the figure was a dragon.

"What is this place?" I whispered.

"It's a mithraeum," Ewan said. "A temple to the Roman god Mithras."

"Why is there a mithraeum under Agent Hunter's ancestral home?"

"That, Princess Pendragon, is a very good question. The cults of Mithras were very secret, underground. The Society has some records on them, but not much," Ewan said then shook his head. "When the Romans left, they took their gods with them. The teachings of Christ came into fashion not long after, and all the old gods were nearly forgotten."

"Nearly forgotten."

Ewan nodded. "Some of the Celts reverted to the old religion. Some converted to Christianity. But others had converted to the Roman gods whose cults are still alive and well. The Cult of Mithras," Ewan said then let out a long whistle. "Very secret."

I glanced around the room. "Look," I said, pointing to one of the reliefs on the wall. On it was a crumbling castle tower. Men stood looking at the tower, gesturing at its failing state. At the front of the crowd was a man and a boy. And under the tower were two dragons. Though the paint on the relief had faded, I still spotted the faint glow of red on one dragon, white on the other.

"Vortigern's castle," Ewan and I said at once.

I smiled at him. "You know the story?"

He nodded. "Of course. Vortigern's new castle kept falling apart as they attempted to build it, so he called for the most powerful magician in the land to come and determine why. Merlin was just a boy then, but everyone knew he was a gifted seer. It was Merlin who revealed that two dragons— one white, one red—were at war under the castle. Only once the dragons were set free could the castle construction continue."

"Set free or killed," I said, "depending on who's telling the tale."

Ewan nodded.

"Why this image here? In a temple of Mithras?" I asked.

Ewan shook his head. "Vortigern was Roman, perhaps a follower of Mithras. I don't know. Maybe the story was just a metaphor."

"Or maybe…" I said then took the torch from Ewan's hand. I approached the lion-headed statue. I eyed it over, paying close attention to the depiction of the dragon. The man. The lion. The dragon. They were in symbiosis. The three together. One. What did it mean?

A soft breeze blew in from one of the side corridors. And

along with it, I heard a faint voice sing that same melody: *I'm the spirit of them all.*

"Let's see what's down there," Ewan said, turning toward the cavern. He pulled another torch from the wall, and we followed the narrow passage to the next chamber.

It felt strange to be in a cave once more. It was like being at home, yet the sense of confinement was frightening. My hands trembled as I considered my future. After all this, I could never survive being shut away again.

The passage let out into another chamber with a tall domed ceiling. At the center of the room was a round altar. I looked up. The stone overhead glimmered in the torchlight.

"Altar or table?" Ewan asked.

I touched the surface of the stone then shook my head. "I don't know."

Ewan shrugged. "Mithras was known for feasting rituals. And we all know that round tables lead to good things, right? I mean, no one makes human sacrifices on a round table. That's just uncouth. And certainly not in Britain."

I chuckled then nodded.

"Shall we?" Ewan said, motioning toward the exit.

Ewan and I left the table chamber then crossed the temple to the other side, where we entered the second corridor. As we walked, it soon became apparent that this passage led away from the temple. As we went, we passed seven different mosaics. Each had different symbols. Spades, moons, crowns, and sickles, amongst other items were depicted. Though I didn't understand their meaning, I could feel the weight of the magic on me. The worship of Mithras had become part of the realm's history, part of what made up Britannia. I felt its energy. We followed the narrow passageway until we reached yet another flight of stairs carved from the bedrock. As we ascended, we discovered a stone covering the exit. Ewan scanned the wall until he spotted a lever. He pulled it then motioned for me to step back. A moment later, the stone slid away. Fresh, night air poured in from outside. Extinguishing our torches and leaving them behind, Ewan and I headed outside.

We found ourselves standing in a Roman-style domed gazebo in the rose garden. Heady red roses covered the edifice. Once we were both safely out, Ewan and I scanned around, looking for a means to close the grate. Rather than vertical Roman columns, the gazebo dome was held aloft by statues of the Roman gods. Under the light of the moon, I studied them all until I found the lion-headed figure from the temple once more.

"Here," I said, pointing to the statue.

Ewan eyed it over then reached out and touched the key that the statue held in its hand. Moving carefully, he turned the key.

There was a scrape as the stone grate closed.

Ewan turned and looked at me. "Well, that was unexpected."

"And what did you expect to find down there?"

Ewan shrugged. "Guns? Gold? Not sure, but not a secret temple of Mithras."

I chuckled. "Never know what you'll find in a cave."

He stepped closer to me and set his hand on my waist. "No. Indeed not," he said then very slowly pulled me toward him. "Rapunzel," he whispered.

"Yes?"

"I have something I have to tell you," he whispered, staring into my eyes.

"O-okay."

"I… I love bacon too."

I grinned. "I know."

Ewan leaned toward me, setting his other hand on my

cheek. I closed my eyes. Kissed in the rose garden of my own, personal Pemberley. Could there be anything more perfect?

Then a massive explosion erupted, rocking the ground around us. I heard the glass in the windows of the manor house shatter. My eyes snapped open, and I turned in time to see a whoosh of orange light shoot up into the sky from the front of the house.

I turned back to Ewan. "The girls. I need to get to the girls. The egg! I left the egg behind."

Without saying another word, Ewan and I raced back toward the house.

22
AS ABOVE, SO BELOW

We rushed back inside to see three angry-looking dragon bloods burst through the front door.

"This way," Ewan said, leading me down a narrow hall to the servants' staircase. We rushed up the stairs and headed down the hall toward my bedchamber.

There were shouts coming from below and then there was another explosion. Grabbing hold of the balcony rail, I looked over in time to see two more of the dragon bloods enter. That's when the shooting started.

Lucy appeared from the side room, pistols in both hands, and began firing.

"Jesus, Mary, and Joseph," William said as he rushed down the hallway toward us, buckling his belt with one hand and pulling a sword from his back with another. "Looks like they found us. Ewan, get her out of here."

"But you and Lucy—" Ewan began in protest.

"Get Rapunzel and her dragons away from here. I'll go. Can't let Lucy have all the fun," William said then pulled his sword.

Ewan eyed William's blade. "Taking a sword to a

gunfight?"

"Oh, this is new. Got it from the tinkers," he said then activated a lever on the pommel. The sword sparkled blue. I could feel heat emanating off of it. William inclined his head to me then turned and ran toward the commotion.

Ewan and I headed back toward my chamber.

I flung the door open only to duck a moment later as a fireball came blasting toward me.

Wink clicked loudly, alerting Estrid to stop.

Estrid snorted, exhaling a puff of flame.

"Girls, we need to go. Now," I said.

Ewan raced across the room, grabbed the satchel with the egg, and handed it to me. I strapped it on then motioned for the girls to follow us.

"This way," Ewan said, leading us away from the battle underway and toward another servant's stairwell.

Luna clung to my hair as we raced away, Estrid and Wink hovering nearby.

"My auto is parked in the barn," Ewan told me.

"But Lucy and William…"

"Lucy and William have made the same oath as me. They're buying us time. Let's go."

I rushed along behind Ewan. We raced down the stairwell, which ended not far from the kitchens. On the other side of the door, I heard dishes clatter, breaking as they fell to the floor, then a loud scream. It was Caroline, the lady's maid. I listened to a rough, angry voice shouting and Caroline's weepy replies. I felt the hairs on the back of my neck rise. They wouldn't dare hurt an innocent girl, would they? Anger rippled through me.

"Ewan, we need to help," I said, stepping toward the commotion.

"No. We need to get to my auto. Rapunzel, this way," he said, but when I wouldn't budge, he turned and looked back at me. "Rapunzel?"

Glaring down the hallway, I stopped. "We need to help," I said again. This time, I felt sure of it. My body felt strange. It was like warmth was uncoiling from somewhere deep within me.

"I know you want to help, but think about the girls, the egg. We need to get you away from here. If not for your sake, for theirs."

I stared at the door. I could distinctly hear a man shouting and Caroline's frightened cries.

Estrid growled low and mean. I looked from her to Wink. Estrid jerked her head in the direction of the kitchen.

The girls and I headed toward the kitchen door.

"Rapunzel," Ewan whispered, aghast.

Pushing the door open, I saw signs of a struggle. Broken china lay all over the floor. A massive man, a dragon blood, had lifted Caroline by the neck of her dress and was holding her against the wall. The tearful maid was shaking her head.

"I don't know what you're talking about," she sobbed.

"Put her down," I said, my voice sounding far sterner than I ever thought I was capable.

The man stiffened then turned around. Yanking Caroline around him, he lifted a knife off a nearby counter and held it to her throat.

"Lower your gun, Ewan," the dragon blood hissed. "Or I'll cut her throat."

I turned and looked behind me to see Ewan standing there, his pistol aimed at the man.

I nodded to him.

Frowning, Ewan looked from the dragon blood to the maid then to me. He lowered his gun.

"Let her go, Cheron," Ewan told the man.

"Gladly," the man replied then pushed Caroline. She banged against the counter with a grunt. Fear in her eyes, she turned and fled the room.

"You shouldn't have done that," I growled.

"Why not, blood of Anna? What is she to me?" he said.

Glaring at him, I motioned to Wink.

The little dragon blinked. The air in front of the dragon blood shivered, and Wink appeared before the man.

"What in the name of Mordred?" he whispered, but he didn't have time to finish his thought.

Wink exhaled a massive cloud of pink smoke in his face.

At once, the man collapsed.

"Okay, now we really need to go," Ewan said.

Turning back the way we'd come, we raced down the hallway then slipped out a side door. We headed toward the barn. As we raced toward the building, two massive brutes emerged. They ran away from the structure. A moment later, there was a loud explosion, and the barn was engulfed in flame.

"My auto," Ewan whined.

Grabbing my hand, Ewan and I turned and rushed toward the garden.

"Five miles west of the field where we picnicked is a road. We'll head there," he said, but just as we turned the corner, two more of the dragon bloods appeared.

"Ewan, we were looking for you," one of the dragon bloods called. He was the same man from the platform, the one who'd shot the tower guard and the pilot. "Where are you headed with our mate?"

Mate?

"Look," the second man—the one with the odd gun from the airship platform—said. "Dormad, look. Not at her, or Goodwin, at *them*."

Dormad, who had been glaring menacingly at Ewan, turned his attention first to me and then to Wink, Luna, and Estrid.

"Are those...dragons?" he asked in an astonished whisper.

Ewan looked at Wink. "We're going to need that stinky breath of yours again."

The air shivered, and a moment later, Wink appeared in front of the second man.

"Owyr, meet Wink," Ewan called.

Wink snorted then huffed a breath of pink smoke at the dragon blood.

"What the hell?" Dormad called.

A moment later, Owyr fell to the ground.

"We need to go," Ewan said.

I nodded to Estrid. "Get rid of him," I said, motioning to Dormad.

Estrid clicked happily, and a moment later, she let out a massive ball of fire. And then another and another. Dormad, for all his bravado, turned and ran.

"Let's go," Ewan said, and we rushed toward the garden.

Estrid appeared a moment later looking very pleased with herself.

We raced down the path and had just reached the statue of Diana when a gunshot rang out overhead.

Luna chirped nervously.

"Stop," a voice called commandingly.

When we turned to look back, we spotted five dragon bloods coming out of the manor. One held Lucy tightly, her hands behind her back. I didn't see William. Fear, and then anger, washed over me. They hadn't killed him, right? I mean, they wouldn't kill him, would they? The dragon bloods had their pistols trained on Ewan and me.

Estrid hovered in the air beside me. I could feel the heat as she readied a fireball.

"Let her go," I yelled.

"Come with us, blood of Anna, and no one has to get hurt," the leader called. He was a massive man, taller than the others, but also older. He had black hair with streaks of silver at the temples. Like the others, he had a heavy brow and a dark, angry countenance.

"Morad," Ewan replied. "You're a fool. The Once and Future King's true heir will never consort with the likes of you."

"Shut your mouth, Pellinore. God, will someone please shoot him," Morad said, motioning to the others.

Estrid moved between Ewan and the dragon bloods and let out such a terrible roar that they all froze. Even my own body quaked at the sound.

Suddenly, the other dragon bloods didn't look so sure anymore.

Morad sneered then turned to me once more. "Blood of Anna, you are revered amongst my brothers and me. You and your dragons. We are all the children of Pendragon. You are one of us, not one of them. That man is a dragon hunter," he said, pointing at Ewan. "And you are a dragon, like us. They are using you. Don't believe anything the Society has told you. These Pellinores... All they have ever done is hunt us. Come with us, and we will keep you safe. We will honor and worship you. Together, we are the true rulers of this realm. Come with your own kind."

"Show me you mean it. Let Lucy go," I said.

The leader motioned to the others, who shoved Lucy hard. She stumbled as she walked forward, but she didn't fall. Her lip and nose were bloody, and there was a dark mark under her eye, but she was alive. She joined Ewan and me.

"Now, come with us," Morad said, motioning to me. "No one has to get hurt. Let's leave together."

The wind whipped across the rose garden, carrying with it a sweet melody in the air, a soft sound like what I imagined a harp to sound like. And with it, I heard whispered words: *Above. Above.*

I looked from Lucy back to the dragon bloods—and then above them.

Coasting in slowly, the propeller off and lights out, an airship was dropping from the clouds. At the rail, I saw a figure wearing a red cape that billowed in the breeze.

"Rapunzel," Ewan whispered, "don't do it. You can't trust them. They will…mistreat you. Please, don't listen to them."

"You must give your word that no one will be harmed," I told Morad.

Hanging from my braid, Luna chirped nervously in my ear. Estrid looked back at me, giving me an angry, frustrated look. To make her stance clear, she went to Ewan and landed on his shoulder.

"You have our word," Morad said.

I turned to Ewan.

"Please don't do this," he whispered. "Rapunzel, I…"

"You're my butter upon bacon too. No, better than that. But you better get ready, because as above, so below." I winked at him.

A moment later, a gunshot rang out. This time, it wasn't the dragon bloods doing the shooting. As the airship lowered toward the yard, more than a dozen agents dropped from the sky, including Agents Hunter and Louvel.

"Rapunzel," Ewan whispered in shock.

But there was no time. A moment later, a massive brawl began. Fighting his way through the crowd, Morad pushed toward Ewan, Lucy, and me.

"Go," Lucy said, pulling one of Ewan's guns from his holster. "I'll hold him off. Get them away from here."

She moved to engage Morad.

"Come on," Ewan said, and we raced away from the scene.

But a moment later, Dormad appeared in front of us, a massive knife in his hands. "You think you're getting out of here alive, Pellinore? Think again."

"Rapunzel," Ewan called. "The maze then back to Mithras."

Understanding, I nodded then rushed into the hedge maze. At night, the maze felt ominous. I could just make out the tip of Diana's arrow in the moonlight. Following that, I made my way through the maze.

"She went into the maze. Go after her before the agents catch up," I heard one of the dragon bloods yell.

I heard the crunch of gravel as people entered behind me. The sounds of gunfire and fighting fell behind. Luna chirped nervously. With every step I took, I felt like I was making the wrong decision. What was I doing in the maze? I needed to go back and help the agents. I needed to stop the dragon bloods. But how?

My heart thundered in my chest.

I stopped and listened. I heard footsteps coming in my direction.

"She's in here somewhere," a rough voice called.

"We need to grab her and get out of here. The red capes are tearing up the place," another voice answered.

Frowning, I turned and went forward once more. I held the satchel at my side, feeling the egg lying safely inside. I rushed through the dark maze, checking the skyline for Diana's arrow. The walls of the shrubbery, so bright and green in the summer daylight, loomed over me menacingly under the moonlight. I made turn after turn until finally, I spotted the exit.

"Come on," I whispered to the girls, and we rushed out of the maze. Now I just needed to double back to the other side of the garden and slip into the passage to Mithras' temple once more. No one would even know we were there.

I rounded the corner only to find Owyr standing in my way. But this time, he held a long chain. And at the end of it, trapped in steel, was Gothel.

23
PENDRAGON

"Agent Hunter, Agent Louvel, this way," Ewan called from not far away.

"Come with me now, or I'll cut her throat," Owyr seethed.

"Mother," I whispered. Gothel wilted under the heavy steel. There were burn marks on her wrists and neck.

"Rapunzel," Gothel whispered.

The dragon blood struck her hard.

Estrid's tongue flickered with fire.

"Now, blood of Anna."

I stared across the garden toward the forest. Fireflies drifted amongst the grass. The wind blew. The scents of roses, pine, wildflowers, and earth filled the air. My blood began pumping hard. I could hear my heartbeat in my ears, and my skin began to warm. When I looked down at my arms, they had taken on an unearthly silver sheen.

"No," I growled.

Owyr lifted his blade and pressed it against Gothel's neck.

The faerie winced as the steel burned her.

"Let her go," I hissed. My blood thundered through my body. My heart beat so loudly it drowned out my thoughts. My hair fell from its ties and fell loosely down my back. In the wind, I could swear I heard the sounds of drums, bagpipes, and harps. A deep, ancient chant called to me.

"I'm not leaving without you and those dragons. Come now," he said, pressing the blade into Gothel's neck once more. Blood dripped down her throat.

Energy tingled throughout my body. All around me, I felt the land. I felt the roots of the all trees in the forest touching one another. I heard the whispers of the ancient oaks as they spoke their secret language. I heard the roses call with their soft, sweet voices. From deep below, in the temple of Mithras, I heard a single, powerful voice whisper, *I am.*

My hair began to fan out behind me. I could see it from the periphery of my eyes, my long locks drenched in silver light. I raised my arms, strands of my hair rising along with them like dragon wings. The energy from the earth, the realm, lifted me.

"Blood of Anna, you belong with us. Come. Now," Owyr said, but I could see the impression on his face, his eyes widening. And more, I saw a glow reflected on his skin, a silvery blue light emanating from me. "Dammit," he swore. He shoved Gothel to the ground then reached out to grab Estrid.

"No," I shouted. Flinging my hands forward, I tugged the magic of the land, pulling into me, directing it through me. I wrapped an invisible fist around the man, freezing him in place, squeezing him.

Estrid blasted Owyr with an inferno. He crumpled to his knees. A dragon blood himself, he wasn't immediately toasted by the flames, but he still writhed in pain.

A moment later, Ewan, Lucy, Agent Hunter, and Agent Louvel appeared. They all stared, taking in the scene.

After a moment, Ewan called, "Estrid, I think you got him."

Estrid gave Ewan a sidelong glance then extinguished her

flame. Lucy raced forward then kicked Owyr over and immediately slapped some cuffs on him.

Agent Louvel rushed to Mother and began pulling off her chains. The agent spoke in a low tone to her. Gothel nodded as she listened then replied in kind, her voice low. What was that all about?

I closed my eyes and released the magic that had served me back to the land once more.

The land and the king were one.

That was the truth of what it meant to be a Pendragon.

The realm and I were interconnected. Its magic was there, waiting for me to call upon it. But that also meant I had a duty to protect what was part of me.

"Rapunzel," Mother called.

The chains that had bound her lying on the ground, she ran to me and gathered me into her arms.

"Mother," I whispered.

There was a crack as the timbers on the barn—which had been burning the whole time—gave way, the roof collapsing into the structure.

"I lent Willowbrook to the Pellinores for one weekend, and you have half of my estate on fire," Agent Hunter told Ewan. Despite the serious expression on his face, there was laughter in his voice.

"Worse, my auto was inside," Ewan added.

Agent Hunter chuckled.

"It was destroyed on the job. Doesn't that make him eligible for reimbursement?" Agent Louvel asked with a smirk, eyeing Agent Hunter playfully.

He winked at her.

"Sir," another agent said, rushing to join us. I remembered seeing her at headquarters. She eyed me then the dragons. She blinked twice.

"Agent Harper?" Agent Hunter answered.

"We've got the others rounded up and cuffed. What should we do now?"

Agent Hunter laced his fingers behind his back and looked from me to Ewan and to the dragons.

"This is the Pellinores' case. Where is Agent Williamson?"

"In the front. He has some of the others *subdued* there."

I exhaled a sigh of relief to learn William was all right.

Agent Hunter grinned. "I see," he said then turned to Lucy and Ewan. "I would appreciate it if the Pellinores would advise the other agents on how your division wants this situation handled. Per your bylaws, of course."

Lucy grinned. "Yes, sir," she said then grabbed Owyr and yanked him to his feet. "Come along, you," she said, pressing a pistol to his back. Motioning to Agent Hunter, she headed back toward the manor, dragging Owyr along with her.

"I need to check on my staff here at Willowbrook and arrange to send a few messages. Then I think we need to talk," Agent Hunter told me.

I nodded.

Agent Hunter and Agent Louvel headed back to the mansion.

The three little dragons went to Mother, chirping and calling to her, rubbing their heads on her neck and hair.

"Mother," I whispered, taking her hands. She had terrible burns on her wrists and neck. "What happened?"

"The werewolves—it was their airship I wanted to charter —turned on me, handed me over to the dragon bloods for a bit of coin. Agent Louvel found me, but we agreed that I would play the part of prisoner. We didn't want them to know we were on to them until the agency could come to help. I stayed to buy Agent Louvel some time. If I'd escaped, they'd have come for you sooner."

"But you're hurt," I said, looking at her wounds.

"I will return to the Otherworld for healing," she said then set her hand gently on Ewan's arm. "Thank you for keeping my daughter safe."

Ewan smiled at me. "She kept us safe."

"She is a Pendragon. She can't help herself," Mother replied.

"But, Mother, if you are returning to the Otherworld, what should I do? Should I come with you?" I asked, knowing even as I asked that it was the last thing I wanted.

Gothel shook her head. "No. This is your world. I cannot protect you forever, and maybe I shouldn't have tried. It is time for you to live."

I looked from Mother to Ewan and then to my girls. "Living free feels too cheaply won. No. I have something better in mind. But I'll need permission first."

"Permission?" Ewan asked. "For what? From whom?"

I smirked. "Well, I am a Pendragon, but I am not the queen. I'll need permission from Her Majesty if I am to serve this realm."

Ewan raised an eyebrow at me.

I grinned at him. "You'll see. And it will be better than butter upon bacon."

Ewan chuckled. "There is only one thing in this world better than butter upon bacon," he said, and with that, he stepped forward, grabbed me gently by the waist, and planted a kiss on my lips.

I closed my eyes and dissolved into his embrace. His lips were soft and sweet, the echoes of ale and biscuits in his mouth, his sweet lemon and lavender scent under the musky tone that was him. My head felt light and dizzy. My knight. My Darcy.

As we kissed, the land around me sang, the pieces of the song I had been hearing snatches of for days coming together, building upon themselves, and slotting into place. Together, they formed one melody: the song of Britannia.

24
THE SONG OF BRITANNIA

ESTRID, LUNA, AND WINK SAT GAZING AT THE EGG, WHICH glimmered in the summer sunlight. Their nest, built from wild-flowers, herbs, and oak twigs was ready, and so was I. The egg sat at the center.

I sat cross-legged in front of the nest. Ewan stood behind me.

Not far away, Lucy and William both waited.

It would work. It was going to work.

"Now, little one, you will wake," I whispered, gently stroking the egg. The surface was warm but felt different, thinner than it had been.

I cleared my throat and then began humming the song the land had given me. Leaving the safety of Merlin's cave had put all our lives at risk, but if Ewan had not found me, if Mother and I had not left, I never would have heard the voice of the realm. I never would have learned the song.

I hummed the first few bars I had heard on the wind then sang the lines the trees, the fields, the flowers, and the land had whispered to me.

I've been the shadow in the cave
I've been the farmer in the field
I've been the maiden of the lake
I've been the spinner at the wheel
I'm the watcher in the wind
I'm the king inside the hall
I'm the warrior on the field
I'm the spirit of them all
I'll be the roses in the garden
I'll be the leaves upon the trees
I'll be the moonbeams on mushrooms
I'll be the earth, bright and green.
I am.
I am.
I am.
I am.
Britannia.

The egg quaked. It shivered again and then a small crack split across it. Ewan's grip on my shoulders tightened in excitement. William and Lucy crept closer.

The birds in the trees nearby chirped merrily, insects buzzed, the wind blew softly. Butterflies drew near once more. The entire field of them surrounded us. The girls began chirping and calling to the tiny dragon inside the egg. The egg shook once more, and then a tiny snout poked out a small hole at the top of the shell. The little nostrils breathed in the summer air, inhaling and exhaling deeply.

"Come out, little one. We're waiting for you," I called.

At that, the little nose retreated, and then the egg began to glimmer with bright golden light. The magic in the air around us hummed, the egg glowing blindingly bright until a moment later, there was a loud clap which made my ears ring. The shell pieces burst away from the egg and there, in a shimmer of white light, sat a newborn dragon.

Luna crept close to the newcomer.

I stared wide-eyed at the tiny dragon sitting in the nest. Its scales were ruby red, its eyes black as ebony. It had a white belly and gold-trimmed wings. And on its head, it had the stubs of two small horns.

"Are those horns?" Ewan whispered, echoing my own thoughts.

"Yes. It's a male," I said, astonished.

Ewan chuckled lightly. "It's a boy," he called to Lucy and Ewan.

The little dragon looked up at him, clicking to Ewan. Ewan knelt and reached out to touch the dragon. To my surprise, he permitted Ewan's touch. Estrid pushed Ewan's hand aside so she and the girls could get closer. Wink, Estrid, and Luna chirped at and rubbed on their newest family member. When the girls had thoroughly loved on the newcomer, Estrid guided the baby dragon with her snout toward me.

I opened my hand and placed it in front of him. "Hello, little one."

The dragon crawled onto my palm and then clicked at me, his voice questioning.

I giggled. "Yes, I am the one who woke you."

The little dragon purred then rubbed his head against me. I petted his scales. He was warm, much like Estrid.

"Now you need to name him," Ewan told me. "I know. What about Arthur?"

I shook my head. "No. I always thought that if I had a son, I would name him Arthur."

"Makes sense. We'll save that name for our boy then. Any other ideas?"

"Wait, what did you just say?"

"Um. Nothing. So, another name then?"

"What about Merlin? After all, he is the last male dragon.

Merlin saved his life. Maybe we should honor Merlin's foresight."

Ewan nodded. "I like it. Lucy, William, come meet Merlin."

I looked down at the sweet little creature. "Welcome to the world, Merlin," I said, then hugged him to my chest.

EPILOGUE
ARTICLE 7, ITEM 22

I SHUFFLED THE PAPERS IN MY HAND AS I MADE MY WAY DOWN the hallway in Willowbrook to the meeting chamber. When I opened the door, the assembly inside rose from their seats, their chairs scraping on the floor, feet shuffling as they came to attention.

Joining them, I stood at my designated place at the table and gazed around the room. Lucy nodded to me. William winked. And at my side, Ewan stood waiting, trying not to beam at me too embarrassingly proudly. I set my fingertips on the worn wooden table. All around its edges, it was engraved with Celtic knotwork. Each place at the table had been carved with a letter and insignia, markers of the knights who'd once stood in that place. It had taken us months to recover it, finally discovering the table hidden in the rafters of a barn. Once more, the round table had reclaimed its true purpose. I touched the faded letter A on the table in front of me. I inhaled deeply, reminding myself that I was a cave dweller no more. I had my own sacred calling, and I would see it through.

"I, Rapunzel Pendragon, do hereby call this meeting of the Knights of the Round Table to order. Please, take your seats," I said, motioning to the others who stood around the circular table. "Let's begin with updates. Lucy?"

"Lady Pendragon, I am pleased to inform you that we have made a discovery regarding the Ring of Dispel in the archives of a library in Brittany. It was transferred abroad. I have booked passage to the States. I'll be meeting with a gentleman at the Smithsonian Institution when I arrive there."

"Very good," I said with a smile then turned to another new recruit, a Scottish agent whose line we had traced back to the house of Lot of Orkney. "Dennis?"

"I am following leads on Gawain's pentangle shield. I'll be headed to Norway next."

"Very good. Thank you." I nodded then turned to William. "And how are my Pendragon brothers?"

"An unhappy crew," William said with a laugh. "But Her Majesty has seen to it they're keeping busy on their little island in the middle of nowhere. Security is tight. Don't worry, Miss Pendragon, we've got them locked down."

"Thank you, William," I said then went around the rest of the table, getting updates from the other agents gathered there until I reached Ewan.

"And Ewan. Tell us, are the Templars cooperating?"

Due to Ewan's family ties to the grail legends, I put him on the case of tracking down the holy grail. This led him to the Templars, who were still alive and hunting the grail themselves. We also learned that they were not quite human. All in all, they weren't bad chaps, unless the moon was full.

"I was able to provide them with some documents from my family's personal library, accounts of the closest descendants of the grail maiden who may have had some knowledge of where the grail was taken after the fall of Camelot. They were very pleased to have it—I think. At the very least, with Agent Louvel's help, they are willing to talk to me, so that's progress."

I nodded. "Thank you."

Casting a glance around the assembled crowd, I felt pride well up in me. "Very well, knights. We will continue our charge to recover the lost artifacts and wisdom of the golden age of Camelot. Her Majesty sends her salutations and thanks to all of you. We are doing the realm's work, and she is pleased with our progress. Now, I believe Willowbrook's kitchens have been working all morning, and dinner will be served very soon. Shall we adjourn?"

The agents—no, knights—knocked their fists on the table.

I cleared my throat then motioned to the others. Together, we intoned: "We are the Knights of the Round Table. May we be generous, brave, and bold. Made greater by the bounty we may give, we are the protectors of our Sovereign and our Realm. Forever, Britannia."

"Now, let's eat," I said with a grin.

At that, the knights left the hall and headed toward the dining room.

I smiled as I watched them go. In the days after the attack, Queen Victoria had come to Willowbrook to see if I was there to usurp her. Once I had assured her that I definitely had no intentions on the throne, no matter my bloodline, I'd made a simple request...to officially re-form the Knights of the Round Table and recapture Camelot, piece by piece. Much to my surprise, she had assented. Even more surprising was Agent Hunter's willingness to let me stay at Willowbrook Park. Since the estate was vast, it would be a good place for the dragons to grow unseen by the general public, and the perfect staging point for my venture.

Ever since that night, everything had been different. I'd spent my entire life locked in a cave waiting for something to happen...but I'd never known what shape that something would take. As it turned out, everything I ever needed lived deep inside of me. I just needed to set it free. I was a

Pendragon. All that I was belonged to the realm. Well, every bit of me except for my heart, which belonged to Ewan.

I sighed contentedly as Ewan wrapped his hands around my waist.

"Suppose they'll miss us if we don't join them right away?" I asked.

"We're not joining them right away? I thought you were hungry."

"I am," I said then turned and gazed at him.

Ewan grinned down at me. "I know that look."

"Really? And what look is it?"

"You're dreaming."

"Of?"

"Mountains of bacon."

I chuckled. "Not quite. Sometimes a lady simply needs her knight. I evoke Article 7, Item 22."

"Are you in distress, Princess Pendragon?"

"Yes, terrible distress."

"Really?"

"I'm very distressed you haven't kissed me yet."

"Ah. Well. Then I must see to that at once." He leaned in and set a delicious kiss on my lips. My body trembled, and I felt that slight dizziness I always got whenever Ewan kissed me. As the kiss grew more passionate, I leaned toward him, my hands roving, a deep hunger burning within me. I was about to suggest that Ewan and I linger a bit longer when an annoyed click sounded nearby. And then another. And then another. And then there was a tiny, terrible roar.

Giggling, Ewan and I pulled back.

Wink, Estrid, Luna, and Merlin hovered not far away. In the few months that had passed, Merlin had already grown as large as Estrid.

"I think someone is hungry," Ewan said, laughing at Merlin's fierce noise.

"Make that four someones."

"Very well, Pendragon horde. Shall we dine?"

Estrid flew to Ewan and landed on his shoulder. Clicking, she nuzzled his chin.

"Hey, that's *my* knight," I told her.

Estrid blew a smoke ring at me.

Ewan offered me his arm, and together we headed toward the dining room. As I gazed up at him, I suddenly realized that not only had I won my own Mister Darcy, but I'd won a Pemberley to boot. And with it, a future for myself that not even the likes of Elizabeth Bennet could have dreamed. Rapunzel Pendragon. Heir to King Arthur. Leader of the Knights of the Round Table. Beloved of Ewan Goodwin. Cave dweller no more.

AUTHOR'S NOTE AND THANK YOU

Thank you so much for reading *Golden Braids and Dragon Blades: Steampunk Rapunzel*. I really hope you enjoyed my take on the Rapunzel fairy tale. Growing up, I devoured anything and everything Arthurian. I read every Arthurian fiction book I could get my hands on when I was in middle and high school. I loved Mary Stewart, Rosalind Miles, and Marion Zimmer Bradley (and was utterly crushed when horrifying details were released about Marion Zimmer Bradley a couple of years ago). My love of Arthurian literature led me to the halls of the Comparative Literature department at Penn State University. I earned a minor in Comparative Literature at Penn State (my major was Psychology) and went on to earn advanced degrees in English Literature. My passion for Arthurian literature and mythology never died. As I set out to write Rapunzel's tale, I knew I wanted to draw on Arthurian myth. And what's better than dragons? Maybe unicorns. Still haven't figured out a good way to work them in just yet. Thus, a backstory for Rapunzel was born.

As for the other story elements, I love Disney's *Tangled*. Flynn Ryder is probably the best "prince" out of all the suitors in the princess movies. I wanted my Rapunzel to have an equally loveable guy, someone not too perfect, quirky enough to fit her. Ewan is a fun character (who may be a little inspired by Ewan McGregor) with a goofy personality all his own. Through him, we are able to see a view of the Red Cape Society that Clemeny (my Steampunk Red Riding Hood) just doesn't see.

You may also notice I was on a Jane Austen kick while writing this novel. I revisit Austen's works every few years. Austen's works are something *all the young ladies* should read. If you have never read Austen before, start with *Pride and Prejudice*. Be sure to watch the 1995 BBC miniseries with Jennifer Ehle and Colin Firth. It's divine.

I have to admit that digging into my roots and exploring old Arthurian tales has druids, knights, and Romans milling about in my head. Let's see if anything comes of all that chatter.

In the meantime, thank you for reading.

Cheers,
Melanie

ABOUT THE AUTHOR

Melanie Karsak is the author of *The Airship Racing Chronicles*, *The Harvesting Series*, *The Chancellor Fairy Tales*, *The Celtic Blood Series*, *Steampunk Red Riding Hood*, and the *Steampunk Fairy Tales Series*. A steampunk connoisseur, zombie whisperer, and heir to the iron throne, the author currently lives in Florida with her husband and two children. She is an Instructor of English at Eastern Florida State College.

JOIN MELANIE'S NEWSLETTER

HTTP://WWW.MELANIEKARSAK.COM/P/JOIN-MY-NEWSLETTER.HTML

Keep in touch with Melanie online.

www.MelanieKarsak.com
Facebook.com/AuthorMelanieKarsak
Twitter.com/MelanieKarsak
Pinterest.com/MelanieKarsak
Instagram.com/karsakmelanie

Check out all of Melanie's *Steampunk Fairy Tales*
Beauty and Beastly: Steampunk Beauty and the Beast
Ice and Embers: Steampunk Snow Queen
Curiouser and Curiouser: Steampunk Alice in Wonderland
Golden Braids and Dragon Blades: Steampunk Rapunzel

The Chancellor Fairy Tales (Modern Fairy Tale Romance)
The Glass Mermaid
The Cupcake Witch
The Fairy Godfather

Ready to go airship racing? Meet Lily Stargazer and her crew in *The Airship Racing Chronicles* (this series contains mature content)
Chasing the Star Garden
Chasing the Green Fairy

Made in the USA
Middletown, DE
26 June 2019